THE GUNSMITH

459

The Imperial Crown

Books by J.R. Roberts
(Robert J. Randisi)

The Gunsmith series

Lady Gunsmith series

Angel Eyes series

Tracker series

Mountain Jack Pike series

COMING SOON!

The Gunsmith
460 – The Traveling Undertaker

For more information visit:
www.SpeakingVolumes.us

THE GUNSMITH

459

The Imperial Crown

J.R. Roberts

SPEAKING VOLUMES, LLC
NAPLES, FLORIDA
2020

The Imperial Crown

ISBN 978-1-64540-239-8

Chapter One

Dimitri Markovich stared at the Imperial Crown of Russia. It was a jewel encrusted golden heirloom that had sat upon the heads of many Russian rulers.

"It is beautiful, is it not?" Tatiana Romanova said, from behind him.

He turned and looked at her as she lay naked in his bed.

"Not as beautiful as you, but it is exquisite," he agreed.

He closed the case that held the crown and walked to the bed. He was also naked, a huge, barrel-chested man covered with black hair that was almost like fur.

Tatiana had long black hair, which shimmered against her pale skin. The patch of hair between her legs was like a forest filled with promise, and her breasts were like ripe peaches.

He joined her on the bed. She reached out and took his huge penis in her hand. It immediately began to swell.

"The Tsar was foolish to send it on this trip," he told her.

"But he has you to look after it," she said. "How could it be any safer?"

"Still," he said, "it is very valuable, even to those who do not know its history."

"Well," she said, stroking him, "it does have lovely jewels on it."

He reached out and placed his large hand against her throat.

"If you even think about it—" he started.

"—you would break my neck," she said, caressing his hand. "I know that, Dimitri. Do you think you cannot trust me?"

"When it comes to the crown," he said moving his hand from her throat, "I trust no one, my sweet." He squeezed her breasts with both hands, hard enough to cause her pain.

"You can trust me, Dimitri," she hissed. "You *can*."

"Here is what I trust you to do." He put one hand behind her head and pushed her down so that his cock was in her face. Then, with his other hand, he slapped her face with the hard column of flesh.

Tatiana did not resist. She knew it would do no good. Dimitri was too strong. That was why he was in charge of the Russian delegation's security.

So she obediently pressed her lips to his hard cock. He released his hold on her head and sat back to enjoy . . .

***

After sex Dimitri always rolled over and slept soundly—like the dead. Only then did Tatiana quit the bed and cross the room to the velvet box which held the Imperial Crown of Russia. It was the intention of Tsar Alexander III to allow the crown to "tour" the United States in an attempt to gain the country as an ally.

She lifted the lid and lost her breath as the crown came into view. It wasn't the Grand Imperial Crown, but the Lesser Imperial Crown. She knew the Grand Crown had 4,936 diamonds and 74 pearls. The Lesser Crown was created along those lines, but on a smaller scale. Still, it was breathtaking. Tsar Alexander III—who came into power when his father was assassinated in 1881—was smart enough to keep the Grand Crown under lock and key.

Tatiana touched the crown, stroking the gold and the pearls, enjoying the smooth surface of both. When she switched her fingertips to the jewels, they felt cold. Dimitri moaned, turning over in bed, and she quickly lowered the lid. When she did, it seemed to her as if the room got darker.

She went back to the bed. Dimitri was still sound asleep, lying on his back, his flaccid penis resting on one thigh. Even now it was huge. She didn't like the sheer size and bulk of it, or the black hair that seemed to cover his body. But he was Lieutenant Colonel Dimitri Markovich, entrusted with the security of the Lesser Crown of Russia. That was impressive to her. So when he asked her to accompany him on his trip to the United States, she said yes, knowing she would have to accede to certain of his requests which were actually demands.

So she got back into bed with him and hoped she would be able to get some sleep before he woke her to ravage her one more time. And she hoped that her plan would ultimately be worth it.

***

Ali Karim Bey stared up at the windows of the rooms the Russian delegation occupied in the Washington D.C. hotel. He knew the crown was in one of those rooms. What he could not believe was that it would soon be in his hands. If everything went according to plan, that was what would happen in the next few days.

Bey had followed the crown there from Russia, hiding in the hold of the ship while the crown sat in a warm cabin. He could have stolen it then. But where would he have gone? Trapped at sea, they would have eventually found him. No, this plan was better. America was so large, that after he stole the crown, they would never be able to find him.

Chapter Two

Count Maxim Ostrakova entered the dining room of the Washington hotel. Normally a man of his stature would have an aide with him, but he chose to travel to the United States without one. It was bad enough the Tsar had burdened him with that dolt, Dimitri Markovich, as his security man.

He spotted his breakfast companion across the room and walked to the table, his uniform and medals attracting much attention along the way. The man awaiting him rose to his feet.

"Good-morning, Count."

"Good-morning, Mr. Drysdale."

The two men sat.

"I hope you slept well," Drysdale said.

"I did, thank you," Maxim said, "although the bed was quite soft. Is this true of all American mattresses?"

"Many of us like them that way," Drysdale said, "but there are some that are more firm."

Drysdale was a small, meek looking man in his fifties, representing the State Department of the U.S. It was his job to see to the comforts of the delegation, particularly the Count.

"Very odd," the Count said. "In Russia we have one kind of mattress for all."

"Well . . ." Drysdale said, unsure how to respond. "Are you ready for your trip across America?"

"If your train is ready," the Count said, "we are ready."

"And the crown? We can offer you security men—"

"I have the finest of Russian security for the crown," the Count said, cutting him off, "but if it will make you feel better, you may send some men along."

"Thank you," Drysdale said, "it would make our President feel much more secure. I'll have the men at the train in the morning."

"Please make certain they have the proper identification," the Count said. "My man Markovich will kill anyone who cannot identify themselves."

"Kill them?"

"Da," the Count said, "he has very little patience."

"Yes, well," Drysdale said, clearing his throat, "I'll make all my men aware of that."

The waiter came over to take their orders.

"What can I get you?" he asked.

"I do not know," the Count said. He looked at Drysdale. "What is an American breakfast?"

Drysdale looked at the waiter and said, "Two bacon-and-eggs, please."

"Yes, sir."

"Bacon-and-eggs," the Count repeated. "It is a common American breakfast?"

"It is."

"In Russia we would have Kasha."

"Kasha?"

"It is . . . in American you would say . . . porridge?"

"You mean, like oatmeal?"

"Da, oatmeal. Or sometimes we have butterbrots."

"And that is?"

"You would say . . . a sandwich." He pressed his hands together. "One piece of bread with butter, or ham, on it."

"So that's . . . half a sandwich."

"These things," the Count said, "they are not plentiful in Russia. Other times we would just boil an egg."

"This'll be better," Drysdale promised.

***

After breakfast Drysdale said, "Well? How was it?"

He had watched as the Russian wolfed down the food.

The Count wiped his mouth with a cloth napkin and said, "Delicious, but decadent. I should not get used to this, for I will not be able to get it in Russia."

"Then don't get used to it," Drysdale said. "You can have something different almost every morning."

"Is that so?"

"Flapjacks, steak-and-eggs, biscuits . . . Just ask on the train. They'll be able to cook you anything."

"I will keep that in mind," the Count said.

"In your position," Drysdale said, "aren't you used to a certain degree of . . . decadence? I mean, being a Count, and all."

"A certain degree, da," the Count said. "But nothing like this." He picked up the last piece of bacon on his plate and popped it into his mouth.

***

Harold Drysdale entered his office, took off his hat and jacket and sat behind his desk. Moments later there was a knock at his door.

"Enter!"

A man entered and sauntered over to the chair in front of Drysdale's desk. He sat, crossed one leg over the other and got comfortable.

"How did breakfast go?" he asked.

"It went fine," Drysdale said. "The Count was very receptive to American breakfasts. I told him he should try everything."

"That's good," the man said. "Flapjacks and syrup should work perfectly."

"Make sure you and your men have your proper identification papers at the train," Drysdale told him.

"What for?"

"The Count's security chief is not above shooting first and asking questions later."

"Don't worry," the man said. "We can handle a few Russians."

"There'll be the security chief and four men," Drysdale told him. "Don't get cocky."

"I'm bein' paid enough to knock the cocky out of me," he said, standing.

"Just make sure you and your men get the job done," Drysdale said.

"Don't worry," the younger man said, as he walked to the door. "We can take care of some Russians."

As the man left, Drysdale couldn't help but think the comment sounded too cocky.

Chapter Three

Two weeks later . . .

Clint rolled over in bed and looked at the woman next to him. They were both naked, and she was lying on her stomach. She was blonde, with pale skin as smooth as silk. He ran his finger down the center of her spine, right into the cleft between her ass cheeks. Then he ran his hands over those majestic globes and she stirred.

Clint slid down and began to kiss her butt, first running his mouth over one cheek, then the other.

"Is that you, Clint?" she asked, sleepily.

"If it's not, then somebody got into my room." He moved his hands up and down the backs of her smooth thighs.

"What a nice way to wake up," she commented.

"If you turn over, I can wake you up even nicer."

She immediately obeyed, turning onto her back. Her large breasts sagged to each side as a result of their lovely weight. He kissed her belly, reached up to squeeze those breasts and rubbed her nipples. Then he moved his head further down and probed her golden triangle of hair with his tongue.

"Oh," she said, moving her legs, "I see what you mean . . ."

He reached beneath her to cup her ass in his hands while his tongue became more active. She gasped and reached down for him, but, in the end, she grabbed two hands full of the bed sheet instead, and held on tight while waves of pleasure ravaged her body . . .

***

Later, the woman watched Clint get dressed.

"I've never done this before," she said. "We only saw each other last night in the café, and we haven't even exchanged names."

"Sometimes it's better that way," he told her.

She sat up in bed.

"Then you've done this before?" she asked. "Slept with a stranger whose name you don't know?"

"There are times when exchanging names makes no sense, since the two people will probably never see each other again."

"So you're leaving town?"

"That's right."

"Well," she said, lying down on her back, "I suppose it's for the best. No names then."

"Agreed."

"But a kiss goodbye?"

She sat up again and he walked to the bed. What was meant as a short goodbye kiss stretched into something much more involved . . .

***

"Okay, this time I really do have to go," Clint said, getting dressed yet again.

"All right, I'll let you go," she said. "But I'll always remember this."

"So will I," Clint promised. "You're very beautiful and special."

She sighed and said, "I hope I meet another man who thinks so."

"You will," Clint said, and left.

***

The town was Lawrence, Kansas, a sleepy little place about thirty-five miles from Kansas City. Clint had managed to spend several days there without people finding out his name. It had been a restful time, especially the last night with the blonde. Well, that hadn't been restful, but it had been enjoyable.

Now his intention was to have breakfast and get back on the trail.

There was a restaurant down the street from his hotel where he had been eating, and there was no point having his final meal in Lawrence somewhere else.

As usual, the place was doing a brisk business. He was shown to the table he'd been using the past few days, and the waiter asked, "Same?"

"Why change now?" Clint asked.

"Comin' up."

The waiter brought him a pot of strong black coffee, followed with a plate of steak-and-eggs, with spuds and biscuits. Clint was halfway through the meal when a man walked in, looked around, then came towards him.

"Aw shit," Clint said, looking up at Jeremy Pike.

"Hello, Clint," the Secret Service Agent said. "Mind if I sit?"

The last time Clint had been involved with the secret service, he'd ended up in Florida, visiting Geronimo in prison, and eating alligator meat. He told himself then he wouldn't have anything to do with them again, at least for a while.

"It hasn't been long enough," he said.

Pike stared at him. Other diners started to look at them.

"Sit down and stop attracting attention," Clint said, "although I know it'll be hard in that suit."

Pike sat.

"What's wrong with my suit?"

"Nothing, if you're in Washington D.C. Which we're not." He leaned forward. "I'm trying not to attract attention."

"So nobody here knows who you are?"

"That's right."

"All the more reason you should talk to me. Your country needs you."

"That's a new low after what happened last time, even for the government. Even for you."

"I know," Pike said. "I'm not happy about it, but that's how important this is."

"Jesus Christ," Clint said. "How the hell did you find me, Pike?"

"It took me a week," Pike said. "But that's part of what I do, Clint."

"I'm in a nothing town in Kansas," Clint said. "Pike, what the hell?"

There was a second coffee cup on the table, upside down. Pike reached out and turned it right side up.

"Mind if I have a cup of coffee?" Pike asked.

Chapter Four

"What's it about this time?" Clint asked. "Sitting Bull's family?"

"Okay," Pike said, "so that Geronimo thing was kind of a mess."

"Kind of?"

"But it worked out," Pike said. "For him and for his family. Thanks to you."

"That's right," Clint said. "Thanks to me."

"And we know that," Pike said, "but this is different."

"Did West send you?"

"Jim doesn't know a thing about this," Pike said.

Clint finished his last bite, pushed the plate away and said, "About what?"

"The Imperial Crown of Russia," Pike said. "Have you heard of it?"

"No."

"It's been around since— since—I don't know—the sixteenth century, I think."

"That makes it pretty old."

"Yeah, well, the Russians were sending it around the United States, putting it on display."

"Why?"

"They're trying to get the U.S. as an ally," Pike said. "So they figured to put their crown on tour."

"Tell me about the crown."

"It's gold, encrusted with jewels—thousands of them."

"How much does it weigh?"

"I've been told nine pounds."

"And why should I be interested?"

"It's been stolen."

"Ah," Clint said. "I hadn't heard anything about it."

"We've kept it quiet."

"I hadn't heard anything about the tour, either."

"It was in the newspapers," Pike said, "but probably not the smaller periodicals."

"I don't have much time to read newspapers when I'm on the trail," Clint said. "So, when was it stolen? And where from?"

"About a week ago," Pike said, "from a train when it stopped in Kansas City."

"How was it done?"

"At gunpoint," Pike said. "Four men boarded the train, knocked out the Russian guards. Shot the Russian chief of security and took the crown."

"Is he dead? The security chief?"

"No," Pike said. "He's a bull. He shrugged it off."

"So you've been looking for the crown for the past week?" Clint asked.

"I've been looking for you for a week," Pike said.

"Then who's been looking for the crown?" Clint asked.

"Dimitri," Pike said. "He's the security chief I told you about."

"He got shot and he's the one out looking?"

"He has his men, and we gave him two of ours, but he has no confidence in them. We need somebody from the U.S. to ride with him, and it has to be somebody he'll respect."

"So tell me exactly what it is you want me to do?" Clint said.

"Ride along with Dimitri, and find that crown," Pike answered.

"So you want me to work for the government . . . again. After last time."

"Not the government, Clint," Pike said. "Your country."

"You've got some nerve . . ." Clint said.

"I've got to have nerve," Pike said. "Unlike you, I work for the government every day, and I do a lot of things I don't like."

"How do you feel about this Russian crown business?" Clint asked.

"Honestly?" Pike said. "I don't agree with it, never did. It was obvious somebody was going to try to steal it once the word got out—and it didn't take long."

"At least you're honest about it," Clint said. "If I do this, where would I start?"

"Dimitri is back in Kansas City right now, on the train with the Count."

"The Count?"

"Count Maxim Ostrakova," Pike said. "He's the man the Tsar of Russia entrusted the crown to."

"Why isn't he out looking for it?" Clint asked.

"You'll have to ask him that," Pike said. "We can leave today."

"You sonofabitch," Clint said, intrigued in spite of himself.

Chapter Five

Clint and Pike rode over thirty miles to Kansas City in relative silence. Pike was satisfied that Clint was actually coming along with him, but was afraid, if he said the wrong thing, he'd lose him.

Clint was also thinking if Pike said the wrong thing, he'd change his mind. The government had not been kind the last time he did a job for them. He had pretty much had to blackmail them into moving Geronimo's family to a safer environment. He was kind of surprised they were coming back to him.

They arrived in Kansas City late in the day. Pike paid to have Eclipse boarded and got himself and Clint each a room at the Summit Hotel.

"I'll take you to see the Count in the morning," Pike said.

"And the security chief?"

"Probably the entire delegation," Pike said. "Do you want to have supper together?"

"No," Clint said. "I'd prefer to eat alone. Why don't we meet in the lobby in the morning, after breakfast?"

"And I assume you don't want company for breakfast?"

"You assume correctly."

Pike understood. It was Jim West who was Clint's long time good friend. He and Pike were "friendly," but after the whole Florida/Geronimo debacle, Clint wasn't happy with anyone from the U.S. government.

"See you in the morning," Pike said, and they went to their rooms.

***

Clint had supper in the hotel's dining room, hoping he wouldn't run into Pike. The man was a good enough fellow, but at the moment he represented the government, and Clint was holding that against him.

After supper he went to his room and thought about Pike's request. He—or the government—wanted him to ride with Dimitri and find the crown. It was more likely they wanted him to babysit the Russian, who may have been a competent chief of security in Russia, but was now in strange, unknown territory.

Clint had recently begun reading James Fenimore Cooper's leather stocking tales of Natty Bumppo. The character was known to European-America settlers as "Leatherstocking." The first book, which he was almost finished with, was *The Deerslayer*. He was sitting on the bed, reading, when there was a knock at the door. He grabbed his gun from the holster hanging on the bedpost and carried it with him to the door.

"Who is it?" he asked, standing to the side, because most hotel doors didn't stop bullets.

"The desk clerk, sir," a voice said. "I have a message for you."

"A written message?" Clint asked.

"Yes, sir."

"Slide it under the door, then."

"I, uh, am to hand it to you, personally, sir."

Who knew he was in Kansas City? The message had to be from Pike.

"All right."

He opened the door and the clerk stared at him myopically from behind his thick glasses. He recalled, as Pike registered them, that the clerk looked on the verge of crying. At the time he thought the man must be upset about something, but now he figured he always looked that way. He also looked older now that Clint had a good look at him, probably in his thirties.

"Here you are, sir," the clerk said.

"Thank you. Wait a moment and I'll give you something for your trouble."

"Oh, that's not necessary, sir," the clerk said. "Have a good night."

Clint closed the door, holstered the gun and looked at the message.

"Please to meet me in room seven soon as you can. Is urgent, about the Imperial Crown."

The handwriting was elegant, like that of a woman, and it read as if written by someone not from the U.S. "Please to meet me . . ." and "Is urgent . . ." in particular sounded foreign.

Clint decided to see who was in room seven, which was just down the hall from him. He pulled on his boots, strapped on his gunbelt, and left his room.

***

There was a knock at the door of his compartment, so the Count put down the pitcher of vodka he was holding and walked to it.

"Yes?"

"It is Dimitri."

The Count opened the door and admitted Dimitri, then walked back to the sideboard and picked up the vodka.

"Vodka?" he asked. "It is American, but it will have to do."

"Da!" Dimitri said.

The Count poured two glasses and handed one to his security chief.

"Where is Tatiana?" the Count asked.

"She wanted to go out and shop in some of the decadent American shops."

"She might be Russian, Dimitri," the Count said, "but she is still a woman."

"Have you heard from the Americans?" Dimitri asked.

"I have," The Count said. "The American agent, Pike, will be bringing the Gunsmith here to . . . help us."

"The Gunsmith," Dimitri said, sourly. "Why do I need someone with a ridiculous name like that?"

"He is supposed to be a legend," the Count said. "The fastest gun in the west."

"Those are just stories," Dimitri said. "Silly stories of a decadent country."

"Their government wants you to ride with him to find the crown," the Count said. "They are being generous allowing us to use him. That is how they looked at it. And the Tsar wants us to cooperate while we are here. So you will ride with him."

Dimitri looked unhappy about the order.

"Very well, but he will know that I am in charge!"

"That will be between you and him."

"When do we meet him?"

"Pike will bring him here tomorrow morning," the Count said. "You will be . . . civil, Markovich."

Dimitri tossed hack his vodka and said, "Da!"

Chapter Six

Clint knocked on the door of room seven.

"Come in," a voice said.

Prepared for some kind of trap, Clint turned the doorknob with his left hand and pushed. He saw a woman, and a bed, and nothing else.

"Come in, Comrade," the woman said. "We are quite alone." She was sitting primly on the end of the bed, wearing a blue nightgown.

Still ready for anything, Clint stepped into the room and looked around. She was telling the truth; they were alone, so he was free to turn his attention solely on the woman in front of him.

She was a dark-haired beauty with pale skin and blue eyes. The nightgown she wore showed her to be well-shaped, small but solid breasts. The thing he found arresting about her, though, was her mouth. It was full and sensual.

"You may close the door," she said. "That is, if you are Clint Adams."

He reached behind him and closed the door.

"I am," he said.

"Good," she said. "I was hoping you would respond to my message."

"Your accent," he said, "is it Russian?"

"Very good," she said, smiling.

"And you're with the Russian delegation that came here with the Imperial Crown?"

"Again, you are correct."

"So, why are you here?" Clint asked. "Or, more to the point, why am I here?"

She stood up.

"I asked you to come because I was curious," she said.

"About what?"

"The Count and Dimitri—I am sorry. Count Maxim Ostrakova and Lieutenant Colonel Dimitri Markovich. They are the men I travel with. I heard them talking about the American legend called The Gunsmith. And so I became curious."

"And was that the first time you heard the name?"

"Oh no," she said. "We have been in this country long enough for me to hear the names of many legends. Let me see, there was a Wild Bill . . . Hickok, is it?"

"It was," Clint said. "He's dead."

She studied his face.

"He was a friend?"

"He was."

"Then I am sorry I brought him up."

"That's okay," he said. "Who else have you heard of?"

"Wyatt Earp?" she said. "And . . . Bat . . . was it? Masterson?"

"That's right."

"Are they also friends?"

"They are."

"And what sort of name is Bat?"

"He prefers it to Bartholomew."

"Ah. Well, I heard the names of these legends, but the one that seems to be spoken with the more reverence is the Gunsmith. Clint Adams."

"Reverence?" he asked.

"That is what I heard, Comrade."

"Comrade," Clint said. "Is that what Russians call each other?"

"No," she said. "We call each other Tovarich. But others, like you, we call Comrade."

"I'd prefer you call me Clint," he said.

"Very well," she said. "Clint. I am Tatiana."

"I've never heard that name before," he said. "It's beautiful."

He closed the space between them and took hold of her shoulders.

"You're beautiful," he said.

"I think my mouth is too big."

"It's just right . . . for me."

He kissed her.

Chapter Seven

Her mouth was so perfect for him that he kissed her a long time, leaving both of them breathless. Clint enjoyed long, deep, wet kisses and, obviously, so did Tatiana.

"I can already see why they call you a legend," she said.

"Let's see if I can impress you further," he said.

He surprised her and carried her to the bed. Before he put her down on it, he said, "If this wasn't what you had in mind, tell me now."

"Oh no," she said, "this is exactly what I had in mind."

He set her down on the bed, took off his gunbelt and hung it on the bed post. Then he sat on the bed to remove his boots. As he did, she got on her knees behind him, unbuttoned his shirt and slid her hands inside and began to kiss his neck.

When his boots and shirt were off, he turned and took her into his arms. They kissed again, long and deep, and, while they kissed, he pulled her nightgown down from her shoulders to her waist, baring those firm breasts.

As he kissed and nibbled at her nipples, she wriggled the nightgown off completely, then attacked the belt of his pants. Together they got them off him, and his hard cock sprang into view.

"Oh yes," she said, "you will impress me further, with no doubt."

They rolled onto the bed together, their limbs intertwining, trapping his hard penis between them. Her flesh was smooth and hot, her legs powerful as they wrapped around him.

He moved his mouth from hers, kissed her neck, her shoulders, and her breasts, as she cradled his head and moaned her approval.

Clint slid one hand between her legs and found her wet and ready, so he decided to mount her now, then driving his hard cock into her with ease. She moaned aloud and spread her legs to accommodate him. He came to his knees, grabbed her hips and began slamming himself into her . . .

***

"I am impressed," she said later, as they lay side-by-side.

"I'm glad," he said. "So tell me, what are your duties, as far as the crown is concerned?"

"The Count is in charge," she said, "Dimitri is the head-of-security. I am . . . a courtesan, I suppose. What would you call it in this country . . . a whore?"

"I don't believe that," he said.

"What else would you call me?" she asked. "Dimitri asked me to come along. I stay with him, lie with him— he ruts like a pig and falls asleep. I have no other duties."

"Then maybe you should ask for some," Clint said. "Let them know that you're not a whore?"

"Am I not?" she asked, looking at him. "You can say that after I lured you here."

"You didn't lure me," he said. "You asked me here to secure Russian/American cooperation."

"Oh?" she said. "And have we cooperated?"

"We have," he said, reaching for her, "but maybe not enough."

"It will have to be enough," she said, scooting away from him and off the bed. "I must get back to the train."

"Is that where they're staying?" Clint asked. "On the train?"

"Yes," she said, grabbing her clothes and getting dressed quickly. The nightgown she had brought along was tossed aside. When she was done, she looked ready to ride, in britches and boots.

"You will come to the train tomorrow?" she asked.

"That's the plan."

"We will have to pretend not to know each other," she said.

"We can do that," he said.

She went to the bed to kiss him, then rushed to the door.

"I will see you tomorrow."

"Yes."

She didn't leave.

"What is it?"

She turned to face him.

"You must be careful of both the Count and Dimitri," she said. "They are not honorable men."

"It must be difficult for you to say that," he said.

"I am betraying them, yes," she said, "but I already see that you are more of a man than they are. Just . . . be careful."

"You do the same."

She opened the door and was gone.

Chapter Eight

Clint lingered over his breakfast in the hotel dining room, wondering if he was doing the right thing. That is, the right thing for him, not the U.S. government. When Pike walked into the crowded room, Clint ignored him. Let the secret service agent find him on his own, he thought. Pike stood in the doorway, looked around and finally started over to him.

"Good-morning," Pike said.

"'morning."

"Mind if I sit?"

"You don't have to," Clint said. "I'm finished." He stood. "We might as well get going."

"I just wanted to talk a bit about—"

"Let's talk on the way," Clint said, and headed for the door.

***

Pike did his talking in the carriage they took to the railroad station.

"The Count's kind of got his nose in the air," he told Clint.

"That means we won't get along," Clint said. "I hate those people."

"I know," Pike said, "they're not my favorite, either, but we have to put up with it—"

"You do," Clint interrupted, "because you're the government. I don't."

"Okay, well, just do your best not to shoot him."

"I can't promise anything," Clint said.

"Yeah, well . . . then we might have a problem with Dimitri."

"Lieutenant Colonel Markovich?"

Pike gave him a quick look.

"How'd you know that?"

"I have my sources."

"If information is leaking out—"

"It's not," Clint said. "My source is very close-mouthed."

"Are they?" Pike asked. "They talked to you—"

"Pike," Clint said, "don't worry about it. "Let me ask you a question."

"Go ahead."

"What are the chances this is an inside job?"

Pike hesitated, then said, "There's always that possibility. While you're out riding with Dimitri looking for the crown, I'll be back here looking into that."

"Ah, so you already suspect somebody."

"Not specifically," Pike said, "but there were enough people on that train for it to have happened."

"Including your own," Clint said.

"That's true, there were some of our men involved," Pike said. "I'm looking into every possibility."

"Who else is in the Russian delegation?"

"They have a few of their own security men," Pike said, "and I believe there's a woman."

"A woman?" Clint said. "What are her duties?"

"That's unclear. It'll be part of my investigation."

"So you'll investigate while I hunt," Clint said.

"That's the way it's set up."

They rode the remainder of the way in silence. Pike still seemed bothered by the fact that Clint had a "source," which gave Clint some satisfaction.

***

The Russian delegation rated a private train. It reminded Clint of the train his friend Jim West used: just three cars behind the locomotive. The carriage pulled to a stop right next to it, and they got out. Clint noticed men standing guard at each car, including the locomotive. They were large, powerfully built men wearing red uniform jackets, and staring straight ahead.

Pike led Clint to the second car, where he told the guard, "This is Clint Adams. He's with me."

The guard stared at both of them for a few seconds, then stepped aside.

"Thank you," Pike said.

The guard remained silent.

As they stepped up onto the car Clint asked, "Do they speak?"

"I've never heard them, but apparently they understand English."

Pike knocked on the door of the car and, after a few moments, it opened. Clint saw Tatiana standing in the doorway. Their eyes locked, but neither of them reacted.

"Who is it?" a voice called from behind her.

"It is Comrade Pike, with another man."

"Let them enter," the gruff voice called.

Tatiana did not smile at them as she stood aside and allowed them to step in. They were immediately fronted by a large, bull-like man. He was wearing a suit rather than a uniform, but Clint could see in his stance that he was military.

"Your guns, Comrade," the man said.

Pike looked at Clint.

"That's going to be a problem," Clint said.

Chapter Nine

"Dimitri—" Pike started, speaking to the man.

"You go no further until you give up your guns," Lieutenant Colonel Dimitri Markovich stated.

"Let them pass," the gruff voice said. "I am sure we can trust them with their guns."

Dimitri Markovich did not look happy about it, but he allowed them to pass.

The car was plushly furnished in a lot of velvet, green and gold. There were curtains on the windows, and expensive sofas and armchairs scattered about.

Sitting at a round wooden table with a drink in his hand was a dapper looking man wearing a purple jacket with an insignia on it. Clint assumed this was Count Maxim Ostrakova, and that the insignia had something to do with his title.

Markovich came and stood behind them. He had an imposing presence, while the Count's was commanding. For that reason, it was obvious who was in charge.

"Mr. Pike, good-morning," the Count greeted, rising to his feet. The two men did not shake hands.

"Count," Pike said.

"And I assume this is the famed Gunsmith you have with you?"

"My name's Clint Adams."

"Ah," the Count said, "Mr. Adams, I am Count Maxim Ostrakova. It is indeed a pleasure to meet you."

Clint was surprised when the Count extended his hand, but he recovered quickly enough to shake it before the situation became awkward.

"Please, sit," the Count invited. "Vodka?"

"Not this early," Pike said.

"No thank you," Clint said.

"Coffee, then."

"Yes," Clint said, and Pike nodded, "that would be fine."

"Tatiana, will you please bring our guests some coffee?" the Count asked, although it sounded more like an order.

"Of course, Count," Tatiana said.

"Comrade Adams," the Count began, "Comrade Pike has indicated that you have agreed to assist us."

"Actually, I'm still making up my mind," Clint said.

"Ah, then I hope this meeting will help you to do that," the Count said.

"We'll see."

"Indeed," the Count said.

Tatiana came over with a tray bearing a pot of coffee, two cups, cream and some sugar cubes. Both Pike and Clint took the coffee black. She then withdrew.

Pike looked at Clint and raised his eyebrows. The Secret Service man wanted him to take the lead.

"Count," Clint said, "I need all the facts about what happened, and I need to see where the crown was taken from."

"We were ten miles outside of Kansas City when four men boarded the train."

"Or they might have already been onboard," Dimitri said, speaking for the first time.

"Dimitri will tell you what happened and show you where the crown was taken from." The Count waved a hand at his chief of security.

"This way," Dimitri told Clint.

Clint stood and followed the man. Dimitri led him through a small kitchen and out into the next car, which had sleeping compartments. They entered one, which was larger than any Clint had ever seen. It seemed the railroad car had been renovated to have two compartments, rather than eight.

"The four men drew guns, knocked out my guards, and shot me."

"You look pretty good for a man who was shot."

"It was not a bad wound," Dimitri said, "but I was unable to stop them. They came in here and took the crown from there."

He pointed at what looked like a velvet box. Clint went to it and lifted the lid. It was empty.

"How did they know where it was?"

"That is a good question," Dimitri said.

"Weren't there some American soldiers onboard?"

"There were four," Dimitri said. "We don't know what happened to them. They might have been killed and thrown off the train."

"Why wasn't there a whole regiment accompanying you?" Clint asked.

"We did not feel we needed a regiment," Dimitri said. "We felt sure we could handle any situation."

"And you were wrong."

Dimitri firmed his jaw. Clint could see a muscle jumping in the man's cheek.

"It seems so."

"How did they get away?"

"They took horses from the stock car."

"The soldier's horses?"

"It would seem," Dimitri said, again.

"I'd like to see the stock car."

"This way."

Dimitri led Clint to the stock car and stood back while he looked around.

There were two more horses there, probably for inci-dental use by the Count or Dimitri. There were bales of hay against one wall. Clint went to them, poked around, and came up with something.

"What is that?" Dimitri asked.

"Soldier's uniforms," Clint said, dropping them on the ground. "Four of them."

"I do not understand," Dimitri said. "They stripped the soldiers, killed them or threw them off the train?"

"No," Clint said. "They didn't strip and kill the soldiers. They *were* the soldiers."

Chapter Ten

"They what?" Pike asked.

"The crown was taken by the four soldiers," Clint said.

"How—"

Clint dropped the armful of soldier's uniforms onto the floor.

"A lieutenant, a sergeant and two corporals," Clint said.

"Yeah, that's who was assigned," Pike said. "I was there when they boarded. You don't think they're dead?"

The Count, Dimitri and Tatiana waited for the answer, watching from the side.

"There's no blood on any of the uniforms," Clint said, "and none in the stock car. You're sure they were genuine soldiers?"

"Definitely," Pike said. "I knew the Lieutenant, a fella named Edders."

"American soldiers," the Count said. "The crown was stolen by American soldiers. My Tsar will not be pleased, at all."

Pike looked at the Count.

"Don't tell him," he pleaded. "We'll get it back." He looked at Clint. "Won't we?"

"You got their names?" Clint asked.

"I do."

Clint looked at the Count.

"We'll get it back."

"*We* will get it back," Dimitri said, stepping closer.

"Look Colonel—" Clint started.

"Call him Dimitri," the Count said. "It will be easier."

"Dimitri," Clint said, "there's going to be a lot of hard riding—"

"I ride," Dimitri said. "I am a soldier."

"—and some shooting."

"I shoot."

Clint looked at the Count.

"Dimitri is an expert marksman," the man said. "I assure you."

Clint looked at Pike.

"This was the deal," Pike said.

"No others," Clint said, "just me and Dimitri."

Pike looked at the Count.

"Count?"

"Agreed," the Count said. "Dimitri?"

"Agreed," Dimitri said.

"Get yourself one of the horses from the stock car and meet me outside," Clint said.

"Da."

Dimitri left the car.

"The Tsar expects to hear from me by telegram in two weeks," the Count said. "You have that long to find the crown and bring it back."

"Two weeks?"

"That is all."

Clint looked at Pike, who shrugged helplessly.

They left the car together.

Outside Pike said, "If we don't get that crown back—"

"We?"

"Okay, you," Pike said, "If you don't bring the crown back in a week there's going to be a hell of an international incident."

"They have a week's head start, Pike," Clint said. "That crown could have been taken apart and sold in pieces, by now."

"They're not stupid," Pike said. "They know the value of the crown. They just have to find the right buyer. But if they don't have the crown anymore, find out who does. And get it back."

"I'll need their names, and any information you can give me about them."

"I'll bring it to your hotel."

"In two hours," Clint said. "I want to get going."

"Two hours?"

"You better get to a telegraph office."

"Jesus."

"Leave me the carriage," Clint said.

Pike turned and hurried away on foot.

Clint was about to leave when the door to the car opened and Tatiana came out.

"Clint," she said. "I'm glad I caught you."

"Aren't you taking a chance?" he asked.

"The Count doesn't care where I go or what I do," she said, "and you sent Dimitri for a horse." She didn't come down the steps of the car. "I just want to tell you to be careful."

"I intend to," Clint said. "I'm chasing four trained American soldiers."

"No, I mean, be careful of Dimitri," she said.

"What do you—"

At the sound of a horse approaching she turned and hurried back into the car. Clint saw Dimitri riding toward him, wearing a red uniform jacket and a fur cap with ear flaps tied on top.

"Do you really need that hat?" Clint asked.

"It is my *ushanka,*" Dimitri said.

"And the red jacket?"

"This is my uniform," Dimitri said. "It is who I am, and I must wear it while I search for the crown."

"Yes, all right," Clint said. "You can follow me back to my hotel."

Chapter Eleven

Clint took the carriage back to his hotel, followed by Dimitri on his horse. The Russian attracted a lot of attention in his uniform and hat. When they reached the hotel, they went inside to collect Clint's belongings from his room. He tied his bedroll and picked up his saddlebags and rifle. Then he put them back down and faced Dimitri.

"Dimitri," Clint said, "I don't think we want to attract a lot of attention just by riding into a town, do you?"

"Probably not."

"Then I think we need to get you some new clothes."

"But this is my uniform—"

"I understand that," Clint said, "but in this case I don't think the uniform is a good idea. For one thing, it makes you a perfect target."

"What would you prefer me to wear?"

"I assume you have money?"

"I have some."

"Let's make one stop before we leave town."

***

A half hour later, Dimitri was decked out in Levi's, a blue shirt, a brown fur-lined sheepskin jacket, and even a pair of new boots. It was late Autumn, heading into Winter, so the jacket would be necessary. In fact, Clint bought himself one just like it.

Outside the store, Dimitri looked down at himself and said, "This is better?"

"This is *much* better."

Clint collected Eclipse from the livery stable, saddled and mounted him while Dimitri marveled at the Darley Arabian.

"We have fine horses in Russia, but never have I seen one such as *this*."

"Yeah," Clint said, "he's sort of one of a kind."

Once Eclipse was saddled, they rode back to Clint's hotel. Although he had checked out, he was still waiting for a message from Pike. He checked with the desk clerk.

"Oh yes, sir," the clerk said. "It just came in." He handed Clint an envelope.

Outside the hotel he opened it and took out one sheet of paper with four names on it, and a few lines of information for each.

"What is this?" Dimitri asked.

"This is the information on the four soldiers."

"It tells us where they live?"

"Where they came from before they signed up," Clint said. "But I doubt they've each gone home."

"Why not?"

"Because they'll stay together until they've disposed of the crown."

"Disposed?"

"Sold it," Clint said. "They might break it down for the jewels and the gold, but it's probably worth more if they sell it as is."

"And who would buy such a thing?"

"That's the question," Clint said. "A collector, maybe."

"A collector of crowns?" Dimitri asked, frowning. "There is such a person?"

"There are people who collect many different things," Clint said. "Oddities, which this Imperial Crown might be considered."

"Yes," Dimitri muttered, "the Imperial Crown."

"Did I say something wrong?" Clint asked.

"No, no," Dimitri said. "Uh, do we have everything we need?"

"Everything we need to get started, yes," Clint said.

"What will we do first?"

"I want you to take me out to the exact place the four men stopped the train and stole the crown." Clint mounted up and looked at Dimitri. "Then we'll start from there."

***

Dimitri guided Clint back along the tracks until they reached the point where the four soldiers had stopped the train.

"You're sure it was here?"

"Yes."

Clint dismounted and walked the tracks, looking on both sides, then stopped.

"You have something?" Dimitri asked.

"It was a week ago, but I assume nobody else has been here since then," Clint said. He pointed to the ground. "There *are* some tracks here."

"Can you follow them?"

"I don't know," Clint said, "but there is a shoe here with some odd markings on it. It'll be easy to identify, if and when we catch up."

"If?"

"Providing they don't switch horses, somewhere."

Clint mounted up again.

"It looks like they headed North," he said, "so we'll go that way, as well, and see what happens."

He started off, with Dimitri trying to keep up with Eclipse.

Chapter Twelve

One week earlier . . .

Lieutenant Paul Edders stepped into the stock car, where the three men under his command were waiting.

"Kansas City's about ten miles ahead," he said. "It's time."

The three men looked at each other.

"If anybody's gettin' the jitters say so now," Edders said.

"You sure we can get away with this, Lieutenant?" Sergeant Ray Bailey asked.

"I got it figured, Sergeant," Edders said. "That is, unless you wanna keep livin' the way you have the past twenty years, knowin' you're never gonna get more than those three stripes."

"Naw," Bailey said, "I'm sick of bein' called sergeant."

"You fellas?" Edders said, looking at the two younger men, both Corporals.

"We're with ya, Lieutenant," Corporal Peter Gillespie said.

"Just say when," Corporal Chris Lee said.

"I'm sayin' it now," the Lieutenant said. "When . . ."

***

When it was done, the four men entered the stock car again. They were carrying the crown, and in a hurry. The Russian guards had been knocked unconscious, and the security chief had been shot.

"That was not part of the plan," Lieutenant Edders said to Sergeant Bailey. "You didn't need to shoot the Colonel."

"I been itchin' to put a bullet in him since we met," Bailey admitted.

"You didn't kill 'im," Edders said. "Twenty years in the army ain't taught you when you shoot a man, you kill 'im?"

"I can go back and finish him," Bailey offered.

"No time," Edders said. "Let's get these uniforms off, and those horses saddled."

Edders put the crown down and started undressing. They had left shirts and Levi's behind the bales of hay. Once they were dressed, they saddled the horses.

"Get that door open," Edders ordered.

Corporal Lee slid the door wide open. They all saddled up and jumped their horses out of the car. Edders had the crown hanging from his saddlehorn.

The four of them turned and looked back at the train.

"We shoulda killed 'em, Lieutenant," Bailey said.

"No," Edders said, "that would make us murderers *and* deserters. They'd be trackin' us forever."

"You don't think they will be now?" Bailey asked.

"For a while," Edders said. "Once we sell the crown and split the money, we'll go our separate ways."

"How long's it gonna take to sell it, Lieutenant?" Lee asked.

"I've got a feller in St. Louis," Edders said. "He knows somebody, but I don't know how long it'll take. Let's just get there."

The Lieutenant and the two Corporals turned their horses to head off, but the Sergeant still stared at the train. He wanted to go back in and finish the job.

"Bailey!" Edders shouted. "Let's get a move on!"

Bailey turned to look at the younger man.

"We ain't in the army anymore, Edders," he said. "You ain't in charge no more."

"I am until we sell this crown," Edders said. "Then you can go your own way."

"Bailey stared at him. The Corporals were in their late twenties, but Edders was in his mid-thirties. That still made him ten years younger.

"Edders—"

"Besides," Edders said, "those guards are probably wakin' up about now. We better git."

He turned his horse and rode off, followed by the two Corporals. After a few moments, Bailey turned his horse and followed . . .

***

St. Louis
One week later . . .

Paul Edders entered the hotel room he was sharing with three other men. He tossed his hat aside and sat in one of the two red armchairs.

"You don't look happy," Chris Lee said.

"No word yet?" Pete Gillespie asked.

"No, not yet," Edders said, tightly.

"What's the hold up?" Bailey demanded. He was the most impatient of the four.

"The buyer isn't here, yet," Edders said.

"Well, when is he gettin' here?" Bailey asked.

Edders looked at him, then looked away.

"Probably another week."

"What?" Bailey squawked.

"I know, I know," Edders said, "but it can't be helped. He's comin' from somewhere back East."

"Goddamit, Edders!" Bailey snapped. They had long since stopped referring to each other by their former rank.

"Relax, Bailey," Gillespie said. "It ain't his fault."

"Can't you find another buyer?" Lee asked.

"Yeah, what about that?" Bailey asked.

The four men seemed to have split into two factions, Edders/Lee and Bailey/Gillespie. Edders was glad he had Lee; the young man seemed to be the better of the three. He listened and could handle his gun.

"I tried," Edders said. "And I'm still tryin'."

"Well, we're runnin' out of funds," Bailey said.

"If you'd stay out of the saloons and whore houses, you'd have some money left," Edders said.

"So what am I supposed to do, just sit up here with you three?" He stood up. "And speakin' of the saloon." He strapped on his gunbelt, which was still military issue. They were waiting for the money from the crown so they could outfit themselves.

"Wait for me," Gillespie said, following Bailey out the door.

"Those two are gonna be a problem," Lee said.

"I think you're right, Chris," Edders said. "Yes, I believe you are right."

Chapter Thirteen

They rode all day in silence. Dimitri apparently didn't want to talk, and Clint didn't mind. The Russian rode well, and while his horse was not the quality of Eclipse, he kept up. Clint was concentrating on finding some sign that the four men had passed.

When they camped, they spoke only for Clint to tell Dimitri to build a fire while he took care of the horses. Then Clint made coffee and some beans, which he had left in his saddlebags from his previous time on the trail.

"This is how you eat when you are—what do you say—on the trail?"

"This is it. Sometimes bacon. Other times you'll keep a cold camp and just chew on some beef jerky, wash it down with water."

Dimitri grumbled.

"Why, what do you eat on the trail in Russia?" Clint asked.

"Luckily, I do not have to go out on the trail," Dimitri said.

"Lucky man."

"Do you not like it? Being on the trail?"

"Oh, I like it fine," Clint said, "but it's not for every-one."

Dimitri fell silent as he ate his beans. When he was done, he set the plate down and sipped his coffee, then looked at Clint.

"How long will we continue to ride north?"

"We have no other choice, Dimitri," Clint said. "If we keep going, we'll end up in St. Louis. That's a likely place for them to try and sell the crown."

"But they are a week ahead of us."

"I'm hoping they didn't have a buyer waiting," Clint said. "But if they did, that kind of a purchase would have to leave a ripple effect. Somebody will have heard something."

"I do not understand your methods," Dimitri said. "We have the names of these men. Why don't we check their homes?"

"The army was their home," Clint said. "You want to go to the places they were born?"

"They might go home," Dimitri muttered.

"Pike is supposed to be investigating," Clint said. "He'll probably send somebody to each place. I intend to stay on this trail."

"Are you truly able to see a trail?" Dimitri asked. "After a week."

"In some places, yes," Clint said. In his mind he was wishing he was a better tracker. He wished he had the eyes of someone like his late friend, Bill Hickok, or maybe Tom Horn. But he was going to have to do the best he could with the ability he had. Luckily, he had learned long ago to look for that one hoof print that had an identifying mark on it.

"You ready to turn in?" Clint asked.

"Not quite," Dimitri said.

"Then I'll make another pot of coffee."

When it was ready, they each had a cup, and sat for a short time with their own thoughts before speaking again.

Clint could imagine how Dimitri was feeling well out of his normal environment and was probably trying to get used to it.

"What's on your mind, Dimitri?"

"My thoughts are private," the Russian said.

"Not when you're out here with me," Clint said. "I have to know that you're ready for this, ready to back me when the time comes, as I'll back you. That means we need to know each other."

The Russian stared over the fire at Clint, who noticed that the man had the wherewithal not to stare into the fire and damage his night vision. That alone was a good sign.

"Talk to me, Dimitri," Clint said. "I need to know what you're thinking."

Dimitri pondered Clint's request for a few moments, then nodded.

Chapter Fourteen

"I hate your country," Dimitri said, "I hate your people, and I hate you."

"That's honest," Clint said.

"The fact that four American soldiers stole the crown proves I am right to hate you," the Russian went on. "And now I must hunt them and kill them for what they have done."

"I thought our goal was to get the crown back," Clint said.

"I will get it back," Dimitri said, "but I will also kill the four men who took it."

"Well, now," Clint said, "we usually only hang men who have been found guilty in a court of law for committing murder."

"We have heard of your—what do they call it—your 'necktie parties?' Your lynching's."

"Those things do happen, but for the most part we follow the letter of the law," Clint said. "That means I won't stand by and watch you kill these men."

Dimitri gave Clint a hard look, one that Clint was sure struck fear into the hearts of the men he commanded.

"You will not stop me," the big Russian said.

"I guess we'll see about that when the time comes," Clint said. "Can I turn in without worrying about you killing me in my sleep?"

"That is another thing I hate about you Americans," Dimitri said. "Your humor."

Dimitri got up and stalked over to his bedroll.

Clint had another cup of coffee before turning in with his gun close by.

***

In the morning Clint woke to the smell of coffee, which surprised him. He didn't expect the Russian would perform such a menial task.

As he approached the fire, he asked Dimitri, "Do you want some breakfast?"

"I would rather get an early start," the Russian said.

"Fine with me," Clint said, and poured himself a cup of coffee. He was surprised that it was strong like he preferred it.

"I think we're going to stop in the first town we come to," Clint said.

"Why? They would not find a buyer there."

"I doubt they were outfitted when they left the train," Clint said. "If they stopped for supplies, we'll know we're on the right track."

"That makes sense," Dimitri said, after a moment.

Dimitri saddled the horses while Clint killed the fire and packed his saddlebags. Clint heard Eclipse objecting to the way Dimitri was handling him, but the Russian finally got the big Darley saddled.

"He is very willful," Dimitri said, walking Eclipse over to Clint.

"Yeah, he's got a mind of his own."

"Perhaps," Dimitri said, "he is just getting old."

"Aren't we all?" Clint said, mounting up.

***

Clint was annoyed by what Dimitri had said about Eclipse. because he had been thinking the same thing, lately. Eclipse was getting to that age where most horses were put out to pasture. He was a year older than Duke had been when Clint had sent the big gelding out.

The problem was, what could he possibly replace the big Darley with? Where would he find another horse like him? He had lucked out with Duke and Eclipse. Duke had been given to him by Jesse James, and Eclipse by P.T. Barnum. Could he luck out again and find a third horse of that caliber?

But that was something he would have to consider when he had more time to devote to it.

"What is the next town?" Dimitri asked.

"There's a town called Blue Springs, another further on called Odessa. I'm not sure which one would have the supplies they'd need to outfit themselves. We'll have to stop at both."

"Blue Springs," Dimitri said, in disgust. "What a decadent name."

"Well," Clint said, "from what I remember, it's not a very decadent town."

"I was talking about the name," the Russian said.

"I know."

***

They rode in silence until they reached Blue Springs. It had a small mercantile store, but, according to the clerk, four men had not come in for supplies during the past week. They mounted up and continued on.

"Odessa is a much better name," Dimitri said. "Do you know there is a city called Odessa in Russia?"

"No," Clint said, "I didn't know that."

"Blue Springs," the Russian uttered, shaking his head.

"Let's hope we have better luck in Odessa," Clint said.

Chapter Fifteen

Dimitri groused again about the beans, about Americans in general, and about the U.S. government in particular.

"Why did your Tsar choose you for this job, Colonel?" Clint asked, while they sat at the fire. The Count had told him to call the man Dimitri, but he didn't feel comfortable with that.

"He knew he could trust me to keep the crown safe," Dimitri said.

"So when the Count contacts the Tsar, he's going to be real disappointed in you, isn't he?"

Dimitri's jaw tightened.

"Not when I get it back," he said, tightly, "and make the men who took it pay."

They didn't talk much more after that.

Now, as they approached Odessa, Clint said, "This town looks big enough to have the right store."

"You see?" Dimitri said. "A better name, a better town."

Clint didn't know how to respond to that, so he remained silent and headed for Odessa . . .

***

As they rode down the main street, Clint spotted the mercantile. It was a good sized one, where a man could outfit himself with whatever he needed.

They reigned in their horses in front of the store, dismounted and went inside.

"This is good," Clint said. "We can outfit, too, while we're here."

"We do not have a . . . what do you call it . . . pack horse?"

"We won't need one," Clint said. "We'll buy just enough for the two of us to carry."

"Help you fellas?" the clerk asked, from behind the counter. He had just finished with a small, thin woman and her little boy, who bustled past them. She stole looks at Dimitri while trying to keep her eyes front, but the boy stared openly at the big Russian while sucking on a peppermint stick. Even without his red jacket, the big Russian attracted attention.

"Yes, we need a few things," Clint said, pleasantly. "Some coffee, beef jerky, beans, peaches, a slab of bacon, some ammunition . . ."

Dimitri remained silent while Clint had the man put their purchases into two gunny sacks that could be tied closed. But then the Russian became impatient.

"Did you see four men come through here last week?" he asked.

"Eh? What's that?" the old clerk said, putting his hand to his ear. "Come again?"

"Four men—" Dimitri began to tell, but Clint put his hand out to try to calm him down.

"We're looking for four men who may have come this way and stopped here to make some purchases," Clint said.

"I ain't seen four men," the clerk said.

"Well," Clint said, "they may not have all come into the store. Did you see one or two men who bought enough supplies for four?"

"There was two strangers in here last week," the man said, "bought a lot of things. I asked 'em about it, and they just about bit my head off."

"What'd they look like?" Clint asked.

"One was a tall feller in his thirties who acted like he was in charge. The other one—the one who yelled at me—was a burly gent in his forties, with a—" The man waved his hand in front of him. "—red face. He didn't like the other one's attitude."

Clint looked at Dimitri, who nodded.

"Did they happen to say where they were going?" Clint asked.

"They wuz bickering like two hens when they walked in," the clerk said, and pondered it for a moment. "But I didn't hear what it was about, and then they stopped and started jawin' at me."

"You didn't happen to watch them when they mounted up, did you?" Clint asked.

"I watched 'em when they went outside, but they didn't mount up. They walked their horses across the street to the saloon."

"We're much obliged, sir," Clint said. "How much do I owe you?"

Clint settled the bill, and then he and Dimitri each picked up a sack and left the store.

"It was them," Dimitri said. "I recognize the description of the red-faced sergeant. The other description can fit the Lieutenant."

"So now that we know they were here," Clint commented, "let's see if we can find out where they were going when they left."

"How do we do that?"

Clint pointed to the saloon across the street.

"You want a drink?" he asked.

Chapter Sixteen

The saloon was called the First Drink Saloon. It was less than half full, since it was still early in the day. There were a few men at the bar who moved to the other end when they saw Dimitri. The other men at the bar just looked over at them, then went back to their drinks.

"Get you gents somethin'?" the bored looking bartender asked.

"Two beers," Clint said.

"I would prefer vodka," Dimitri said.

"You're not going to find vodka in a western saloon," Clint told him. "Besides, we're really here to talk, not drink."

The bartender brought the two beers over.

"Maybe you can help us," Clint said. "We're looking for four men who may have come through here in the past week."

"You the law?" the middle-aged bartender asked.

"No," Clint said, "but we're tracking them because they stole something from us."

"What'd they take? Horse? I'll bet they stole some horses," the bartender said.

"No, they took a—" Dimitri started, but Clint spoke over him, which was no easy task.

"What makes you think it was horses?" Clint asked.

"There wuz four men in here last week, arguin' like they wuz married."

"What were they arguing about?"

"One of them wuz givin' orders—you could tell he was used to it—and the others wasn't havin' any. And they was fightin' about wantin' new horses. The one tryin' ta give orders said they didn't have the money for that. He said they'd have to wait til they got to St. Louie."

"St. Louis," Clint said. "They said they were going to St. Louis?"

"Well, the one feller said they'd buy horses in St. Louie, so I guess that's where they wuz headed."

"Thanks very much," Clint said.

As he and Dimitri drank down their cold beers, the man asked, "So wuz I right. It wuz horses?"

"Yup, you were right," Clint said. "They rustled some of our horses."

"I knew it," the bartender said, banging his fist down on the bar.

Clint and Dimitri put down their beer mugs and headed for the door.

"Say," the bartender called out, suddenly puzzled, "if they stole your horses, why wuz they fightin' about buyin' more?"

Clint just waved helplessly as he and the Russian went out the batwing doors.

Outside, Dimitri asked, "Where is St. Louis?"

"About four days ride north of here," Clint said.

"Four days?" Dimitri repeated. "They are already a week ahead of us."

"We'll just have to hope they're waiting for their buyer," Clint said. "That crown is not going to be easy to dispose of."

He didn't know how right he was . . .

***

"He what?" Bailey screeched.

"Take it easy," Edders said. "The buyer backed out."

"Why?" Gillespie asked.

"He said the crown was too hot," Edders said. "He said D.C. is up in arms about it, because having it stolen is going to cause an international incident."

"I don't care what kind of incident it causes," Bailey said. "I want my money. We all deserted because you said we were gonna get rich."

"And we are," Edders said. "Settle down, Sarge—"

"Don't call me that, no more," Bailey said.

"All right, Bailey, settle down," Edders repeated.

"He's right," Gillespie said. "You said we'd be rich. Whatta we do now?"

"Just listen to what the Lieutenant has to say," Lee told him.

"He ain't a Lieutenant no more," Bailey said. "None of us is soldiers no more. We deserted."

"All right," Edders said, "look, I'm already working on getting us a new buyer."

"And how long is that gonna take?" Bailey demanded.

"A day, maybe two," Edders said.

"That crown is hot, and you're gonna get a buyer in another day or two?" Bailey asked.

"Okay, maybe a week."

"We can't stay here another week, Edders," Bailey said. "You know they gotta be out lookin' for us."

"We won't stay here, we'll move around," Edders said. "All we need is to be near a telegraph office."

"So where do we go next?" Lee asked.

"I'm still working that out," Edders said. "Don't worry, men, I've got this. We're going wherever we have to go and do whatever we have to do to sell this thing."

Chapter Seventeen

When they rode into St. Louis, Lieutenant Colonel Dimitri Markovich was chomping at the bit.

"How do we find them?" he demanded of Clint.

"I'm going to have to send some telegrams," Clint said. "I have friends who can tell me who the buyers here in St. Louis might be. Once we know that, we'll find out if they've been approached."

"Who are these men you will be contacting?" Dimitri asked.

"One is named Talbot Roper. He's the best private detective in the country, and he has contacts everywhere. The other is Rick Hartman, a businessman who also has contacts everywhere."

"When do we send these telegrams?" the Russian asked.

"Let's get the horses boarded, and ourselves hotel rooms, and then I'll find the nearest telegraph office."

Dimitri grumbled, but agreed.

***

They took care of the horses and got two rooms at the Mayflower Hotel.

"This place is very decadent," Dimitri complained, as they took the stairs to the second floor.

"Why don't you just sit back and enjoy the decadence, and I'll go out and send those telegrams."

"I will come with you."

"There's no point," Clint said. "There's nothing for you to do."

"I will come with you," the Russian insisted. "I can't stay in this place and wait."

"All right, then," Clint said. "While we're out, we'll get something to eat."

"Knowing you," Dimitri explained, "it will be something decadent."

"My God, Lieutenant Colonel," Clint said, "did you just make a joke?"

Dimitri looked confused.

"I do not joke," he said.

They reached Dimitri's room and Clint said, "Stow your gear and I'll come and get you."

"Do not think about leaving the hotel without me," Dimitri warned.

"I'm right next door," Clint said.

"I will leave my door open," the Russian said.

"There you go," Clint said, "I won't be able to go anywhere without passing your open door." Clint started for his room, then turned and said, "You know, we're going to have to learn to trust each other more."

"I trust no one," Dimitri said.

The rooms at the Mayflower were festooned with flowers, in the wallpaper and in the patterns of the arm-chairs. Clint knew Dimitri would not be comfortable there, but that was beside the point. They just needed a place to stay while Clint searched for some potential buyers. They only had a little over a week left to work with.

Clint entered his own room, set his saddlebags and bedroll down, put his rifle in a corner. He had been in this hotel before, so he actually knew where the closest telegraph office was. He also knew there was a restaurant along the way that he was going to take Dimitri to. He knew the Russian would find it "decadent," but he had become determined to smother the man in decadence for as long as he could.

He left the room, found Dimitri standing out in the hall, looking uneasy.

"Did you even go in?" he asked.

"I looked inside."

Clint looked inside, saw that Dimitri must have tossed his saddlebags and bedroll into the room from the door-way. The Russian didn't have a rifle, just a Russian pistol on his belt.

"It's a nice room," Clint said.

"I will go in," Dimitri said, "when I have to."

"Well," Clint said, "lock the door, and we'll get out of here."

***

The first stop was the telegraph office, where Clint sent his telegram to Rick Hartman in Labyrinth, Texas, and Talbot Roper in Denver. He made arrangements for the replies to be delivered to his hotel.

After that, he took Dimitri to the Stafford Steakhouse, probably the best restaurant in St. Louis. When they arrived, the Russian stood in front and stared at the facade, which featured the name of the restaurant in very stylized print.

He glared at Clint, and before he could speak Clint said, "Don't say it. I want a good steak. If you don't want one, then go find another place to eat."

Dimitri stared at the place again, then said, "No, I will stay with you."

"Well, come on, then," Clint said. "The best steaks in St. Louis are waiting inside."

Chapter Eighteen

Dimitri may have considered the Stafford Steakhouse decadent, but he wolfed down a sixteen-ounce ribeye steak, and then ordered a second one.

Clint made do with a single sixteen-ounce steak, rare as opposed to the Russian's well done/charred. He sent it back the first time and told the waiter to have the cook burn it.

Dimitri pointed to Clint's plate and said, "I can't eat uncooked meat."

"This isn't uncooked," Clint said, "it's rare."

"Your plate is filled with blood," Dimitri pointed out. "It is uncooked."

"Any complaints about the potatoes?" Clint asked.

"They are fine."

They washed their meals down with a glass mug of ice cold beer. When Clint proposed pie for dessert, Dimitri said it was "decadent," but he had a slice— rhubarb, naturally, Clint's least favorite. He had peach. They accompanied it with strong coffee.

When the meal was over, Clint paid and wondered why. The Russian had said he had money, but Clint didn't know how much. He silently vowed to make the Russian pay for some meals. And supplies, if they needed more.

Clint was hoping this search for the men who stole the crown wouldn't go further than St. Louis. If it did, it was going to stretch beyond two weeks, and the U.S. government would have to deal with its international incident. Of course, once that did happen, he would be out of it.

When they left the Stafford, they walked back to the Mayflower. Upon entering the lobby, Clint stopped at the desk to check for telegrams. As he expected, there were two. He knew his friends would not let him down. The only question had been whether or not Tal Roper would be in town to answer his. Obviously, he was.

They carried the telegrams upstairs and both entered Clint's room before he read them.

"We have three names," Clint said. "Let's check a fella named Calvin Prescott first."

"Why that one first?" Dimitri asked.

Clint held up the telegrams and said, "Because his is the only name on both telegrams."

***

Paul Edders entered the shop and waited for the man behind the counter to finish with his customer. He looked around, eyeing the merchandise that was for sale there—pots, vases, large and small sculptures, some jewelry . . . a little bit of everything. The owner was a dealer in many items.

When the customer was gone, he stepped up to the counter.

"Well?"

The man looked away. He was tall, slender, with grey hair that came to a widow's peak and a long jaw.

"He's not comin'," the dealer said.

"What the hell happened?"

"His wife died," the man said. "He has to stay behind to plan the funeral."

"Can't somebody else do that?"

The man looked surprised.

"He'd still have to attend," he said. "It was his wife."

"Well . . . you'd think he'd want to get away from there and forget."

"She only just died."

"Yeah, well . . . now what?"

"I have a couple of other possibilities," the dealer said, "but I'll have to send some telegrams."

"We can't stay in St. Louis much longer," Edders said. "We need a place to lay low."

"There are several towns close by."

"Hannibal, I guess," Edders said.

"Too far," the dealer said. "I might need to get you here quick."

"St. Joe?"

"Also too far."

"Where do you suggest, then?"

"There's a town right across the Missouri called St. Charles," the dealer said. "Go there, find a hotel, and let me know where you are. I'll get back to you as soon as I can."

"You better get this done," Edders said. "I only did this because you said you could find a buyer."

"Believe me," the dealer said, "I want my cut."

"You'll get it," Edders said," if my three partners don't kill me, first."

***

"His wife died?" Chris Lee said, in disbelief.

"That's what the dealer said."

They were in a small saloon having a drink, just the two of them at a table. Edders wanted to tell Lee first, before Bailey and Gillespie.

"Bailey's gonna take this bad," Lee said.

"I know it," Edders said. "That's why I wanted to tell you first, Chris. If I have to make a play, I want to know you'll back me."

"A play?" Lee looked confused.

"Like you said," Edders went on. "Bailey's gonna take this bad. If he goes for his gun—"

"You think he will?"

"He's a hothead," Edders said. "Always has been. That's one of the reasons he's not gone any higher than sergeant. In fact, he's lost his stripes a couple of times."

"What about Gillespie?"

"I'm afraid he'll follow whatever Bailey does," Edders said.

"So whataya want me to do?"

"Keep your eyes on Gillespie," Edders said. "I'll handle Bailey."

"You really think they'll throw down over this?" Lee asked.

"I think it'll be up to Bailey."

"What if we have to kill 'em?" Lee asked.

"Well," Edders said, "then that means we'll only be cuttin' the profits two ways, doesn't it?"

Chapter Nineteen

The next morning Clint and Dimitri stopped just out-side Calvin Prescott's gallery, which was located in a part of St. Louis known as Clayton. There were a lot of other shops and galleries on the street, as well as across the way.

Dimitri looked in the window at the items on display and, before he could say it, Clint said, "I know!" He'd already gone through enough "decadent" comments over breakfast at the Mayflower for one day.

They entered the shop, the inside of which Dimitri observed with distaste clearly etched on his face. There were no customers at that moment, so the man behind the counter came around.

"Help you gents?"

"Are you Mr. Prescott?" Clint asked.

"I am."

"My name's Clint Adams, and this is Lieutenant Colonel Dimitri Markovich."

"Russian army?" the man asked, looking at Dimitri.

"Da!" Dimitri said.

"What can I do for the Gunsmith," the man asked, "and a Russian Colonel?"

"Actually," Clint said, "if you don't already know, you're probably not the dealer we're looking for."

"I don't understand."

"I was told you're an honest man," Clint said.

"Who told you that?"

"Talbot Roper."

"Roper," the man repeated. "He did a job for me a few years ago."

"I know," Clint said. "When I told him I was looking for someone who might be interested in a rare item of great value, he gave me your name. He said if it wasn't you, you'd know who it would be."

The man folded his arms across his concave chest, stared at Clint from behind wide-framed glasses.

"What are we talking about?" he asked.

"The Great Imperial Crown of Russia," Clint said.

"What?"

"It is not the *Great* Imperial Crown," Dimitri said.

"What?" Clint said.

"What's going on?" Prescott asked. "Is it the crown, or isn't it?"

"It is a crown," Dimitri said, "but it is the Lesser Imperial Crown of Russia."

"There are two?" Clint asked.

"Da," Dimitri said. "There is the Greater Crown and the Lesser Crown."

"But they're both worth a lot, right?" Prescott asked.

"Da," Dimitri said, "the Lesser Crown is worth very much money."

"What does it look like?" Clint asked.

"It looks like the Great Crown," Dimitri answered, "just smaller."

Clint looked at Prescott.

"Has anyone come to you, looking to sell a crown?" he asked. "They probably don't know it's the Lesser Crown, so they would have referred to it as the Greater one."

"Well," Prescott said, "nobody has come to me with a Greater or Lesser Crown, so I can't help you." He turned and walked back around his counter.

Dimitri looked at Clint, who knew what he was thinking.

"Just calm down," he said.

"He must help—" Dimitri started.

"Just let me do all the talking," Clint said.

"Make him help," Dimitri said.

Clint walked to the counter.

"Let me ask you the next question," he said.

"Go ahead."

Chapter Twenty

After they left Prescott's gallery, Clint proposed they stop someplace and have a drink. Dimitri objected to every one they passed within blocks of the gallery, so they kept walking until they were out of that artistic area of town. When they came to a small hole-in-the-wall saloon, they went inside.

Despite himself, Clint asked the bartender if he had any vodka.

"Sure."

"Is it Russian?" Dimitri asked.

"Huh? No, I don't think so."

"I will have it."

"And a beer for me," Clint said.

They took their drinks and walked to a corner table. There was only one other customer, sitting at a table alone, moping over a beer.

"What do you plan to do now?" Dimitri asked.

"Well," Clint said, "we could wait."

"How long and for what?"

"Prescott said he'd have some names for us by tomorrow."

"So we will waste the rest of today?"

"We do have two other names," Clint said. He had gotten two names each from Rick and Roper. Prescott's name came from both of them, so that left two others.

"Then we should check them," Dimitri said, "and not waste a day."

"That's all right with me," Clint said. "Maybe Prescott will give us the same names."

"Do you know where to find these other two men?"

"I have an idea," Clint said, "but we need to talk about something first."

"What is that?"

"Why didn't you ever tell me that the crown was the Lesser Crown?" Clint asked.

"It was not my place," Dimitri said. "The Tsar told the Count not to tell anyone when we reached America."

"But he told you?"

"He did not have to," Dimitri said. "I knew it when I looked at it. It is beautiful, but I knew it was the Lesser Crown immediately."

And it's worth a lot?"

"A small fortune."

"But still a fortune," Clint said, "especially for four soldiers."

"Da!"

"Well, I suppose everything else is the same," Clint said. "We still have the remainder of two weeks as a deadline, and your Tsar is still going to be upset."

"Da," Dimitri said, with less enthusiasm. "That is very true."

"Let's get going, then," Clint said, pushing back his chair. "How was the vodka?"

"Awful," Dimitri said.

They both rose and left the saloon.

***

The other name given to Clint by Rick Hartman was a man named Bennigan. He had a store in a much less artsy part of town, loaded with what looked like antiques of all kinds, from pots to furniture to books.

Bennigan himself looked like an antique: small, wrinkled and wizened.

"A Russian crown?" he repeated. "And you say Rick Hartman sent ya?"

"Yes," Clint said.

"And what's your connection with Hartman?" Bennigan asked.

"He's a good friend of mine."

"And you're Clint Adams?"

"That's right."

Bennigan stared at Clint for a few moments, before speaking again.

"I don't suppose you'd lie about a thing like that," Bennigan said. "Claimin' to be the Gunsmith when you ain't. That'd put a target on your forehead."

"Yes, it would."

"And this here fella?" Bennigan asked, jerking his thumb at Dimitri.

"Lieutenant Colonel Dimitri Markovich," Dimitri said. clicking his heels.

"Ah, a Russian."

"Da!"

"Well, I guess I gotta disappoint you boys," Bennigan said. "I ain't heard nothin' about no crown, Grand or Lesser. Wish I did." He smiled. "But maybe I can interest you in something else?"

"Sorry, no," Clint said. "We're only looking for the crown."

As they left, Bennigan said, "Come back if you find it. I'll give ya a good price!"

Dimitri muttered something that sounded like "Mudak." Clint later found out it meant "asshole."

Chapter Twenty-One

The other name Clint got from Talbot Roper was Dakota Wood. Her store was in an area that seemed to be rated somewhere between the other two—not rundown, but not artsy. It was called Laclede and was near the Mississippi.

As they entered the store, Clint ignored Dimitri's reaction. He found the place small, clean and quaint. The lady behind the counter, pretty, in her thirties, with long auburn hair.

"Good afternoon, gentlemen," she said, as they entered her empty store. "What can I do for you today?"

"Are you Dakota Wood?" Clint asked.

"That's me," she said, then with a suspicious look she added, "Who's asking?"

"My name's Clint Adams," he said, "and this is . . . Dimitri." He purposely shortened Dimitri's introduction. "Talbot Roper sent us to see you."

"Roper," she said. "I haven't seen him in quite a while. You a friend of his?"

"A good friend," Clint said.

"Well, then," she said, "What are you looking for?"

"A crown," Clint said.

"What kind of crown?"

Clint looked at Dimitri.

"The Lesser Crown of Russia," the Russian said.

"Oh my," she said, "I heard that was touring the country." She looked shocked. "Was it stolen?"

"It was," Clint said.

"Wait," she said, "I thought it was the Greater Crown."

"So did I," Clint said, "but it was the other one."

"It is still very important that we get it back," Dimitri said.

"I guess so," she said. "Your governments are lookin' at an international incident."

"I'm assuming," Clint said, "that no one has come to you with the crown?"

"No," she said, "I wish they had. I would've bought it."

"And if you did buy it," Dimitri asked, "you would tell us now?"

"Of course."

Dimitri looked at Clint.

"I believe her," Clint said. "Roper said she's honest."

"What you're lookin' for," she said, "are some dishonest dealers."

"Exactly," Clint said. "Do you know any?"

"I know many," she said, "but the man you need to talk to is Calvin Prescott. He'll steer you the right way."

"We've talked to Mr. Prescott, and he's going to get back to us," Clint said. "But anything you could tell us would really help."

"Let me think about it," she said, speaking directly to Clint, "and then you can come back here to buy me supper tonight, and we can talk."

"I could do that," Clint said. Truth be told, he would much rather eat supper with her than the sour Dimitri, again.

"Come back at six," she said. "That's when I close."

"I'll see you then," Clint said. "Thanks."

Clint and Dimitri left the shop and headed back to the Mayflower Hotel.

***

When Clint was ready to leave to meet Dakota, he stopped at Dimitri's room.

"I think you should stay here and let me talk to her alone," he said.

"Why?"

"I think she might have something she wants to say to me," Clint said, "without you around."

"I do not understand," the Russian said.

"I didn't think you would," Clint said, "but take my word for it, I should go alone."

"Then go," Dimitri said. "What will I do?"

"Just stay here and relax," Clint said. "You've been pretty tense this whole way, Dimitri."

"I am never tense," Dimitri insisted, firmly, "I am a soldier."

"I get it," Clint said. "But for tonight, be a soldier in your room. When you get hungry, go down to the dining room, then come back up here."

"You will inform me about what happens, Da?"

"Yes, I will," Clint said. "I don't know when I'll get back, so why don't I come and get you for breakfast."

"As you wish," Dimitri said.

"I have a book I could loan you," Clint offered.

"I do not need a book," Dimitri assured him. "I will be fine."

"All right, then," Clint said. "I'll see you in the morning. Tomorrow we should get something, either from Dakota, or from Prescott."

"I hope you are correct," Dimitri said, "for we are running out of time."

Chapter Twenty-Two

When Clint reached Dakota Wood's shop, it was the first time he noticed it didn't have a name. He entered, found her alone behind the counter, cleaning it with a blue rag.

"You're right on time," she told him. "I'm just finishing up."

"Have you had any thoughts regarding what we talked about?" he asked.

"You know," she said, "you surprise me."

"How's that?" he asked, approaching the counter. There was something else he hadn't noticed earlier. She smelled good. Either he hadn't been paying attention, or she had applied a scent since then.

"I expected the legendary Gunsmith would be a tough and tumble type," she said. "You're much more . . . educated."

"I grew up and was educated in the East, then came west to find my fortune," he said.

"And did you?"

"Not a chance," he said. "All I found was a reputation."

"And you couldn't turn that into a fortune?" she asked.

"I'm still trying."

"Like with the crown?" she asked.

"What do you mean?"

"I mean, if you could get the crown and turn it into cash, would you?"

"I'm afraid not," he said. "I guess I should've told you, I'm working for the government on this."

"Ah," she said. "Well then, you should come into the back. I've got something to show you."

"Like what?" He wondered if she had the crown, after all.

"You'll see."

She walked toward the back and went through a curtained doorway. He followed, ready to draw his gun if it turned out to be a trap.

But as he entered the storeroom, he saw her standing in the center of the room. All around her were dusty, old items—picture frames, furniture, sculptures. And right in the middle of it all, she was undressing.

"Dakota—" he started.

"Now, hear me out," she said. "We were attracted to each other as soon as you walked in. I haven't had a man in my life for some time. I know you've had lots of women, so what's one more notch on your gun?" By this time, she was naked.

She was full-bodied, with bountiful tits and ass. If he wasn't attracted to her as soon as he walked in, like she said, he certainly was now.

She placed her hands on her hips, stared at him and asked, "What do you say?"

He removed his gunbelt and asked, "Are we getting supper after?"

***

Paul Edders sat on the front porch of the Lewis & Clark Hotel, the St. Charles hotel he and the others had checked into. In the next moment, Chris Lee came out the front door.

"How is he?" he asked.

"Bailey's livid," Lee said, "but what can he do? He wants his cut."

"He's not thinking about making a move, is he?" Edders asked.

"You mean making a grab for the crown himself?" Lee asked. "I don't think so. He'd never know where to get a buyer for it."

"Where are he and Gillespie?" Edders asked.

"They went out the back to get somethin' to eat. He said if he came out this way, he might shoot you."

"He's welcome to try," Edders said.

Lee grabbed a chair next to Edders.

"There are a lot of places to eat around here," he said. "We won't run into them."

"Yeah, we'll go in a minute," Edders said. "I just want to sit a while. You can go, if you want."

"Nah," Lee said, "I'll wait. I don't wanna tempt Bailey and Gillespie by leavin' you alone."

They sat in silence for a few moments before Lee said, "Do you think you can trust your man?"

"Like you said about Bailey," Edders said, "my man wants his cut."

"Are you sorry we pulled this job?" Lee asked, after a few moments of silence.

"Hell, no, kid," Edders said. "We're gonna be rich. We just have to be a little patient." He looked at Lee. "Well, a little more patient."

"Patience ain't really Bailey's specialty," Lee pointed out.

"I know." He stood up. "Come on, let's get something to eat."

Lee rose and they stepped off the porch.

"How much longer do you think we're gonna hafta wait?" Lee asked, as they started walking.

Like I said, kid," Edders replied, "we're just going to have to be more patient."

Chapter Twenty-Three

Dakota watched and waited while Clint got undressed and set his gunbelt aside, within easy reach. Then she walked up to him, put her arms around him, pressed her naked body against his, and kissed him.

He put his arms around her, pressed his palms to her smooth back, then slid them down to her powerful butt. Her ass cheeks were very firm as he squeezed them. Her arms were strong as they encircled him. Then she stepped back and took his hands.

"Come with me."

"Wait," he said, and picked up his gunbelt.

"You really think you're going to need that?"

"There's always more of a chance that I will then I won't," he told her, slinging the gunbelt over his shoulder.

She started to pull him by both hands, but he wanted his right hand available, so he pulled it free, still allowing her to continue to tug him by his left.

When they got to the back of the room, he saw a blanket on the floor.

"Is that always there?"

"No," she said, "I don't do this a lot. I put it there after you and your Russian friend left. Where is he, anyway?"

"Back at the hotel."

"So he won't be interrupting us?"

"I hope not."

"Then come . . ."

She got down on the blanket and pulled him with her. He set the gunbelt aside, again.

"Why didn't you just take me home with you?" he asked.

"I did," she said. "This is my home. That is, upstairs, but it's a mess. I didn't have time to clean up. This will do. Besides, with me on my back, this will make for excellent penetration." She reached out to take hold of his hard cock. "When we get around to that."

He took her breasts in his hands. They were as firm as her butt. Her brown nipples grew turgid beneath his palms as he rubbed them. She began to stroke his cock with one hand, cradled his testicles with the other.

"Lie down," she told him, pressing him onto his back. She began to kiss his neck, his chest, his belly, working her way down. Finally, she settled between his legs, kissed his thighs, closed her eyes and pressed his hard penis to her cheeks, enjoying how smooth and hot it was.

She took him fully into her hot mouth and began to suck him. He reached down to hold her head lightly and enjoy himself as he slid in and out. When she had him as hard as he could be without exploding, she released him from her mouth and mounted him . . .

***

Dimitri Markovich entered the Mayflower dining room and was shown to a table.

"What can I get you, sir?" the waiter asked.

"Steak, well done," Dimitri said, "charred, and beer."

"Coming up."

He didn't want to tell Clint Adams that he enjoyed American steak and beer. He didn't want anyone to know he liked such decadence, that he would miss it when he went back to Russia.

If he went back to Russia.

If he and Clint Adams did not retrieve the Lesser Crown, he would not be allowed to live once he got back to Russia. Which meant that, if they didn't get it back, then he wasn't returning to the homeland.

When the waiter brought him his plate and beer, he noticed a woman sitting alone across the room, watching him. When she saw that he was looking at her, she smiled and nodded.

"Who is that woman?" he asked the waiter.

The man turned and looked to see who he meant.

"The one sitting alone," Dimitri added.

"Don't rightly know," the middle-aged waiter said. "Never seen her before, but she's sure good-lookin'."

"Yes, she is," Dimitri said.

"Enjoy your supper," the waiter said, and walked away.

Dimitri began cutting into his steak when he noticed someone standing at his table. He looked up and saw the woman. She had black hair, blue eyes, a wide mouth with some lines at the corners that hinted at her age. He figured she was probably forty or so. She was wearing a black lace dress, and, although he doubted it, she looked as if she could be Russian.

"Hello," she said.

"Hello," he answered.

"I was wondering if I might sit with you," she said.

"Why?" he asked.

"Well, I'm a woman alone, and there are a lot of men in here lookin' at me," she said. "I'd just feel safer sitting with a man of your stature."

"Stature?" the Russian asked. "What is this?"

"Say, where are you from?" she asked.

"I am from Russia."

"Well, hell, that's another country, altogether, ain't it?" she said.

"It is."

"I just mean that you look like a man nobody would cross," she said. "I'd just feel safer eatin' with you."

He studied her for a few moments, then something occurred to him and he said, "Sit."

She settled into the chair across from him and said, "Thank you."

Chapter Twenty-Four

Dakota had been right about the penetration. Sitting atop him, she bounced around and every time she came down her eyes went wide, and he grunted.

Later, when he was on top, driving himself in and out of her, every time he dove in, he went so deep her insides closed around him, almost sucking the seed from him . . .

***

She took him to supper at a place not far from her shop.

"You look like a steak man," she said.

"Exactly right," he said.

"Then this is the place you want in St. Louis," she said.

Above the door it said, RUBY'S STEAKHOUSE.

"I'll let you know," he said, "after we eat."

"Oh, don't worry," she said, taking his arm, "you'll thank me."

"I think I already did that," he said.

***

Dimitri's thought, just before he told the woman to sit, was that he hadn't had a woman since he and Clint Adams left the train. His last time with Tatiana had long since worn off, and he needed a night of sex to get rid of some of the nervous energy he was feeling.

Luckily, the woman, whose name was Sylvia Trench, had the same idea.

"This was what I had in mind," she said, as they entered his room, "when I looked across the dining room and saw you."

Now Dimitri had her stripped naked, and on her hands and knees on the bed. He got behind her, gripped her hips, admired her big ass before driving his big, hard cock up between her thighs and into her soaking, waiting pussy.

"Oh yeah," she gasped, "my Russian bearrrrr . . ."

***

"Well?" Dakota asked, looking across the table, "how is it?"

"After one bite," he said, "pretty good."

"Keep eating," Dakota said.

"I will," Clint assured her, "but let's talk."

She cut into her own steak.

"About what?"

"Dealers in St. Louis who might be interested in the Russian crown."

"Oh, that's easy," she said.

"Tell me."

She put a piece of medium done steak into her mouth, chewed and swallowed, and said, "All of them."

"All?"

"Of course," she said. "We're talking about something of enormous value. The gold, the jewels, the pearls . . ."

"Does that mean if they came to you, you would have bought it?"

"Not me," she said. "I don't have enough money. In fact, none of the dealers do."

"Then whichever dealer they approached will only be trying to find them a buyer, right?"

"Right."

"And how long would that take?"

"A week," she said, "more if the buyer is from the East."

"And is that likely?"

"Oh yes," she said. "I doubt they'd find a buyer here. It would be, oh, New York, Boston, possibly Denver or Sacramento."

Clint doubted it was Denver, or Roper would have known about it. And if the buyer was from Sacramento,

Rick would've known. It would take them both a little longer to find out if it was someone in the East.

"Can you find out who the buyer might be?" Clint asked Dakota.

"You said you've talked to Calvin Prescott?"

"Yes."

"I wouldn't be able to find out faster than he would," she said. "You're better off with him."

"I should hear something from him tomorrow," Clint said. "I was just hoping that I'd be able to get some information from you tonight."

"And you did," she said, "didn't you?"

***

After supper, Clint turned down Dakota's invitation to go back to her shop.

"I've got to be at my hotel in the morning," he said. "There might be something from Prescott."

"I could come with you," she offered.

"I don't think my Russian friend would like that," Clint said. "He's pretty much all business."

Chapter Twenty-Five

Clint returned to the Mayflower Hotel later that night and stopped in front of Dimitri's door. He was about to knock to fill the Russian in on what he'd found out—nothing—when he heard sounds he definitely recognized. Apparently, the Russian had made a friend, so Clint decided to leave Dimitri to it.

He turned in for the night.

***

The next morning, he washed and dressed, walked down to Dimitri's door once again. And once again, he heard familiar sounds from inside. He hoped that the Russian was grunting in pleasure, and wasn't actually tied up, or worse. He decided to knock.

The grunting stopped and he heard heavy steps. The door jerked open and the big Russian appeared with a sheet wrapped around him. Since he had claimed the sheet from the bed, the woman there was totally nude and not shy about it. She actually waved at Clint with a smile, not bothering to cover her very large breasts.

"Sorry to bother you," Clint said.

"Are you going down for breakfast?" Dimitri asked.

"Yes, in the dining room."

"I will meet you there."

"Take your time," Clint said. "Finish what you're doing."

The Russian grunted and slammed the door.

Clint headed down.

***

Sylvia Trench watched Dimitri walk back to the bed and unwrap the sheet from his thick, hairy body. She was very pleased that he was still sporting that huge erection.

"Friend of yours?" she asked, as he joined her on the bed.

"I would not say that," Dimitri answered.

"Then that probably makes me your only friend in town, huh?" she asked.

He grunted roughly, grabbed hold of her and flipped her over . . .

***

Paul Edders came down to the hotel lobby, found Chris Lee waiting there.

"Just us for breakfast?" Edders asked.

"Yeah, Bailey and Gillespie already went out," Lee said.

"I guess they don't want any part of us until we sell that crown," Edders said.

"Where is the crown, anyway?" Lee asked.

"Don't worry," Edders said. "It's safe. Come on, let's eat."

***

Clint had just ordered his breakfast when Dimitri appeared in the doorway of the dining room. He saw Clint and attracted a lot of attention as he crossed the room.

"How's your friend?" Clint asked, as the Russian sat.

"She is just a woman I found last night," Dimitri said. "Not a friend."

"Whatever you say," Clint said, then spoke to the waiter. "I'll do ham-and-eggs."

"Steak-and-eggs for me," Dimitri said. "Burn the steak."

"Yes, sir," the waiter said.

"So, you like our American steak, huh?" Clint asked.

The Russian scowled and said, "It is the best of your decadent food."

"It would be," Clint agreed, "if you didn't have them burn it every time."

"What did you learn from the woman?" Dimitri asked, ignoring the remark.

"Nothing," Clint said. "She's of the opinion that we'll get more help from Prescott than she can offer."

"And where is he?"

"We should be hearing something from him today," Clint said. "Hopefully, right after breakfast."

He had checked with the desk clerk when he first came down, but there were no messages. He hoped it would be different after they ate.

"We do not have much more time," Dimitri pointed out.

"We've got days," Clint said, "relax. And if we can't get back to the train in time, you can send a telegram."

"The Count will want the crown in his hands," Dimitri pointed out.

"You know, the Count will have to take what he can get," Clint said, "and so will my government. Personally, I really don't care what happens to the crown."

"You would risk an incident—"

"An international incident is your government's business, and the United States', it's not mine."

Chapter Twenty-Six

When they checked with the clerk at the Mayflower front desk, they found a message.

"What does it say?"

"Three more names."

"They are buyers?"

"No," Clint said, "dealers."

"Again?"

"According to Prescott," Clint said, "If there's a dealer in St. Louis arranging for the sale of that crown, it's one of these names."

"Then we shall go and see," Dimitri said.

"Yes, we will," Clint said. "I'll wait here while you go upstairs and get your gun."

"Why do I need my gun, when I have you?" Dimitri asked.

"Let's just say I feel better with someone watching my back."

"I will get my gun."

Clint waited in the lobby while Dimitri went upstairs. He was fairly certain the Russian was also going to have to take care of the woman in his room.

Dimitri returned in fifteen minutes with his gun on his hip. That was enough time to fetch it and let the woman out the back way.

"I've been meaning to ask you about that gun," Clint said. "Can I see it?"

Dimitri hesitated, then removed it from his holster and handed the pistol to Clint.

"It's not very heavy," Clint said, hefting it. "Two pounds?"

"Just under two pounds, da," Dimitri said. "Very good."

"How many shots?"

"Seven."

"What's it called?"

"It is the Nagant EM-eighteen ninety-five."

"Eighteen ninety-five?" Clint asked. "That's years away."

"The weapon was made in Belgium for the Russian military," Dimitri said, "It will be mass produced and introduced by eighteen ninety-five. This is an advance model."

"Tell me more."

"It is double-action and has a gas seal system to increase the muzzle velocity."

"Impressive," Clint said, handing it back. "I hesitated to ask you this before, but since we're friends now, I'd like to see you shoot."

"You want me to prove my abilities? You do not trust that I am capable?"

"I'd just like to see the gun in action," Clint said.

Dimitri had replaced the gun in his holster. Now he took it out again.

"Uh, let's wait until we get out in the open."

"As you wish," the Russian said, and replaced the weapon in his holster. "And we are *not* friends."

They left the hotel.

***

They spoke to two of the dealers on the list, both of whom said they had not been approached by anyone about the Lesser Crown.

Dimitri became aggressive, and Clint stepped back and allowed him to frighten the two dealers.

"If we discover that you have lied," he told them, "we will be back, and you will pay. Is that understood?"

Both dealers nodded, staring at Dimitri wordlessly.

"He understands," Clint said, in each case, and they left.

They moved on to the shop of the third dealer . . .

***

"How many such men and women are there in this city?" Dimitri asked, as they approached the third.

"Counting Prescott, we've talked to seven," Clint said. "They seem to be the most likely to handle the crown."

"Then if the other six are not involved," Dimitri said, "it must be this one."

"Or someone else, altogether," Dimitri said.

Clint put his hand on Dimitri's arm to stop his progress.

"What is it?" the Russian asked.

"What you just said makes sense," Clint said. "But if this is the dealer working with Edders and the others, then we shouldn't go barging in there."

"We should barge in," Dimitri said, "so I can beat the information out of him."

"No," Clint said, "Dimitri, I think we should watch him."

"And wait until they contact him, or he contacts them?" the Russian said.

"Right."

"That could take too long," Dimitri said. "Perhaps he will not contact them until he has a buyer."

"Then that's what we should do," Clint said.

"What?"

"Give him a buyer."

Chapter Twenty-Seven

To do what Clint was suggesting, they needed help. He decided to ask Prescott, not Dakota Wood. After all, the man they were targeting was given to them by him.

When Prescott saw them enter his gallery, he excused himself from the male customer he was helping.

"Something else?" he asked Clint.

"Yes," Clint said, "but finish with your customer, first."

Prescott nodded and went back. Clint browsed while Dimitri simply stood and waited. After Prescott walked his customer to the door, he turned the sign on the door from OPEN to CLOSED.

"What's going on?" he asked.

"We talked with two of the names you gave us, and they claim not to have been contacted by anyone about the crown," Clint said.

"And you believed them?"

"Yes."

"Then who's left?"

"This one," Clint said, taking out his list. "Stuart Quincy."

"Are you going to talk with him?"

"We want to watch him," Clint said, and explained his logic.

"To tell you the truth," Prescott said, "he was the one I most suspected."

"Oh? Why?"

"He's the most crooked," Prescott said. "Why did you leave him for last?"

"Just worked out that way," Clint said.

"So what do you need from me?"

"We figure he's not going to contact the thieves unless he has a buyer."

"Ah . . ."

"We want him to hear that there's a buyer in town."

"You?"

Clint nodded.

"Me."

"As yourself, or under another name?" Prescott asked.

"Has it gotten around that I'm in St. Louis?"

"Not really," Prescott said. "This isn't the Old West. People are concerned with their own lives, not with what the Gunsmith is doing in St. Louis."

"That's good," Clint said. "Let's go with another name then."

"Like what?"

"Something that sounds like a buyer from the East," Clint said.

"There's a fella I know has a pretty good reputation for buying objets d'art, but never does the actual buying himself."

"Then I could be working for him."

"Exactly."

"What's the name?"

"Raymond Bonner," Prescott said. "From Boston."

"Well, I'm not from Boston but that doesn't mean I can't work for somebody who is," Clint said. "Can you pass the word that I'm in town, representing him?"

"Sure thing," Prescott said. "What name are you going to use?"

"Let's just go with Clint Adams," Clint said. "I'll say Bonner hired me to buy the crown and safeguard it until I got it back to him."

"Makes sense," Prescott said. "A purchase like that would need a bodyguard."

"Get the word out today," Clint said. "We only have a few days to get this done."

"I'll do it immediately," Prescott said. "If I hear something, I'll get word to you at the Mayflower." Clint started to speak and Prescott added, "I'll try to make it quick."

Clint looked at Dimitri, who raised one eyebrow.

***

As a result of Prescott's help, a telegram was delivered to the hotel in St. Charles, where the thieves were staying.

It was taken to Paul Edder's room, and he called for the other three to meet him in the dining room. Over supper, he told them about the telegram.

"We have a buyer," he said.

"Finally!" Bailey said. "Is he here?"

"He's in St. Louis."

"Make him come here," Bailey suggested.

"Actually," Edders said, "I should've said there's a representative of his in St. Louis."

"Can he make the buy?" Bailey asked.

"I think we'll have to meet with him to find that out for sure," Edders said.

"Here," Bailey said, "in St. Charles."

"I've already sent a telegram to that effect," Edders said. "He'll be here tomorrow."

"Why don't you look happy about it?" Lee asked.

"The buyer's representative," Edders said, "is the Gunsmith."

Chapter Twenty-Eight

"Say that again?" Bailey asked, leaning in as if straining to hear.

"We have to deal with the Gunsmith, Clint Adams," Edders said.

"What the hell does he have to do with this?" Gillespie demanded.

"That's just what I was thinkin'," Bailey said.

"I'm guessin' this buyer wants that crown to arrive safely and he thinks the Gunsmith can accomplish that," Edders said. "Me, I don't care who hands us the money."

"How much are we gettin'?" Bailey asked anxiously.

"We need to meet with him to hash that out," Edders said.

"When's he comin'?" Lee asked.

"I'm waitin' for another telegram, but I'm guessin' tomorrow."

"Then we better be ready for him," Bailey said.

"I'll meet with him, Bailey," Edders said.

"You're gonna need back up," the former Sergeant Bailey said.

"I don't aim to go up against his gun," Edders said, "just his brain, and I think I've got it over him in that department."

"What makes you think that?" Gillespie asked.

"What the hell—" Edders said. "He's a gunfighter, he uses his gun, not his brain!"

***

Clint was pleased he wasn't meeting the dealer at his shop. Instead, the man had invited him to supper, and messaged him where to meet.

The restaurant was called Magnolia's, and obviously dealt in more than just steaks. As he entered, he saw the customers there were well-dressed and, at some tables, entire families sat.

He was told to simply enter and wait inside the door. He did that and a host in a tuxedo approached him.

"Mr. Adams?" he asked.

"That's right."

"This way, please," the host said. "Mr. Quincy is waiting."

"Lead the way," Clint said.

He followed the man across the floor to a table for two near the back, where a man sat, waiting. He had a long angular face, and a hairline that formed a widow's peak. As Clint and the host approached, the man stood, revealing himself to be very tall and slender.

"Mr. Adams?"

"That's right."

"Stuart Quincy," the man said, extending his hand. "Please, sit," he invited as they shook hands.

Clint sat across from him.

"I hope you're not the kind of Westerner who can only eat steak," the dealer said.

"What did you have in mind?"

"They do a wonderful roast chicken here."

"I'll go with that, then," Clint said, "on your recommendation."

"Excellent!" He waved a waiter over. "Two roast chickens, and two white wines."

"Yes, sir," the waiter said.

"You come here often, I bet," Clint said.

"All the time," Quincy said. "So tell me, how did a legend of the West like you get mixed up with someone like Raymond Bonner?"

"He sought me out, contacted me about this crown," Clint said. "It sounded like something I'd like to see."

"Oh, it is," Quincy said. "It's exquisite."

"When do I get to see it?"

"Well, I'm afraid you'll have to go to St. Charles for that."

"St Charles?"

"Right across the Missouri, from here," Quincy said. "It's a fairly artsy little community, quite well known as a Lewis and Clark stopover point."

"Ah, yes," Clint said. "I thought it sounded familiar."

"If you have no objection," Quincy said, "you can ride out there tomorrow and meet with them."

"Them."

"You'll meet a man named Paul Edders," Quincy said. "I'll give you the name of his hotel."

"And how did Mr. Edders get the crown?" Clint asked.

"That's really not important."

"My employer is concerned with the crown's . . . what do collector's call it?"

"Provenance?"

"That's the word."

"Then I suggest you take that up with Mr. Edders," Quincy said. "I'm just a middleman."

"I'll do that."

They stopped talking as the waiter set their suppers down on the table.

"So tell me," Quincy said, "how do you like St. Louis?"

Chapter Twenty-Nine

Clint knocked on Dimitri's door when he got back from meeting with Quincy.

"Come in," the Russian told him, backing away from the door.

"Your friend's not around?" Clint asked.

"She was not a friend," Dimitri said. "I just . . . used her."

"Did she know that?"

"Da, of course," Dimitri said. "She was using me."

"Sounds like a good arrangement."

Dimitri closed the door, turned to face Clint.

"What happened?"

"I'm set for a meeting tomorrow in St. Charles."

"With who?"

"I'm guessing with Lieutenant Edders—or ex-Lieutenant Edders."

"I will come," Dimitri said, "and we will force him to tell us where the crown is."

"Why don't I just go and buy it from him?" Clint suggested.

"We will not pay him—oh, I see," the Russian said. "Let him think you are going to buy it."

"So he'll show it to me," Clint said. "Once I see it, I'll take it."

"What if all four of the thieves are there?" Dimitri asked.

"You'll be nearby," Clint said, "watching my back."

"What is wrong with your back?"

"It's just an expression," Clint said. "It means you'll be backing me up."

"Backing you up?"

"You'll be there to help me in case anything goes wrong," Clint said, making it clearer.

"Ah, da," Dimitri said, "yes I will."

"I'd like to go out early tomorrow morning, though, and get some idea of how you shoot."

"I am a soldier," Dimitri said. "I shoot very well."

"With that gun?" Clint asked, pointing. The Russian pistol was sitting atop the dresser, with its holster.

"With that," Dimitri said, "or a rifle."

"Good," Clint said, "then we'll try you out with my rifle, as well."

"So you want me to prove I can shoot."

Clint hesitated, then took a tact he thought the Russian would appreciate.

"Why don't we say we'll find out who shoots better," he said. "You or me."

Dimitri raised his eyebrows. "We can do that."

***

The next morning, they rode early and headed for St. Charles. Before they reached the bridge that went over the Missouri, they stopped in a clearing.

"All right," Clint said, dismounting along with the Russian. "Let's see what you can do with that pistol."

"What do you want me to shoot?"

"See that tree? About twenty yards away. The lower branch. Can you hit it?"

"That's far."

"Should be able to hit anything inside of forty yards with a handgun. After that you'd need a rifle."

"I could hit a man that far away," Dimitri said. "Let us see if I can hit that branch."

He sighted down the barrel, fired once, missed. Then he fired a second time and hit it, but left a piece hanging.

"Not bad," Clint said.

"Now you," Dimitri said.

Clint drew and fired, almost in one motion. The dangling branch went flying.

"Can you do that again?" Dimitri asked.

Clint drew and fired again, took the rest of the branch off.

"It appears your reputation is well deserved, Adams," Dimitri said.

Clint replaced the two spent shells in his gun before holstering it.

"Do you always do that?" Dimitri asked. "Reload before you return it to your holster?"

"Every time," Clint said. "My gun always sits in my holster fully loaded."

He turned, walked to Eclipse, took his rifle from the saddle.

"Let's see what you can do with this," he said, handing the rifle to Dimitri.

"The same tree?"

"No," Clint said, "there's one about sixty yards straight ahead. See it?"

"I see it."

"Hit any part of it."

Dimitri sighted along the barrel and fired. The bullet struck the trunk of the tree at its fattest point.

"That's good enough," Clint said. "Now me?"

"No need," Dimitri said, returning the rifle to Clint. "I concede you are the better shot."

"As long as you can hit a man at this distance, we'll be fine," Clint said. "Let's mount up. We got a meeting to go to."

Chapter Thirty

Clint and Dimitri crossed the bridge into St. Charles at about noon. The meeting was set for two o'clock. Clint still assumed it was with at least one of the thieves, Paul Edders, since he was the Lieutenant.

The hotel was the Lewis & Clark, on a main street in St. Charles called Riverside Street. It didn't run along the Missouri, but was only one block away from it. The meeting place was the front porch. It surprised Clint that they would be willing to meet him right at the hotel they were staying in.

There was a small park across the street from the hotel. Clint directed Eclipse into the trees and dismounted. Dimitri followed.

"I think you should watch from here," Clint said, "And keep the rifle ready." He handed the Russian the weapon.

"Do you expect all four?" Dimitri asked.

"I expect Edders to meet me on the porch, but I think the other three will be around. Remember, you may be a soldier, but so were they. They're going to set up some kind of a maneuver."

"I will be ready," Dimitri said.

"Good," Clint said, "but we're early, so let's just watch for a while."

***

After an hour Dimitri said, "You are a patient man."

"Rushing headlong into a situation can get you killed," Clint said. "I've seen that countless times."

"You said I was a soldier, and they were soldiers," Dimitri said. "Were you ever a soldier?"

"I was," Clint said, "for a short time, during the war. Since then, though, I've worked for the Army a time or two as a civilian."

"And for your government."

"Yes," Clint admitted, "but these experiences are starting to wear thin. I think this might be the last time I go out of the way for them."

"But if you are called to serve your government," Dimitri said, "how can you refuse?"

"I don't know," Clint said. "I guess I'll just have to wait and see."

They stopped talking at that point and went back to silently watching.

***

Chris Lee was standing at the window of Paul Edders' room.

"What do you see?" Edders asked.

"Nothin'," Lee admitted. "I mean, there are people on the street, but nobody I think would be the Gunsmith."

"None of us have ever seen him before," Bailey said, "so how would you know him?"

"I'm just sayin'," Lee replied, "I don't see anybody who looks like a legend of the West."

"All right," Edders said, "you boys better get down there and take up your positions."

"What about that park across the way?" Lee asked, pointing out the window.

"That's too far," Edders said. "I want you to hear what's being said."

"Why?" Gillespie asked.

"Because if I say the words, that's not how this is gonna go, I want you all to kill the Gunsmith."

"Before he pays us for the crown?" Bailey asked.

"That will mean I don't think he's going to pay us," Edders said.

"So you don't think he's really here to buy the crown?" Gillespie said.

"That's just great!" Bailey grunted.

"I didn't say that," Edders replied. "I just want to be prepared."

The other three men headed for the door.

"Remember," Edders said, "keep apart, and if there's a crossfire, don't hit each other."

"We haven't forgot everything we learned as soldiers, Edders," Bailey said, sourly.

They left the room. Edders was going to give them enough time to get situated.

***

"There they are," Clint said.

He and Dimitri watched as the three ex-soldiers came out of the hotel and split up. They took up positions adjacent to the hotel porch, from when they would be able to see and hear everything.

"Good," Clint said. "None of them are coming over here. You'll have this park to yourself."

"I will not be able to hear anything," Dimitri said. "How will I know when to fire?"

"You're a soldier, Lieutenant Colonel," Clint said. "You'll know."

Chapter Thirty-One

Clint waited in the park until he saw another man come out onto the porch and take a seat.

"Is that him?" Dimitri asked.

"I don't know," Clint said, "but I'm going to find out. I'll ride back up this street, and then make it look like I just got here."

"I will watch from here, and be ready," Dimitri said.

Clint walked Eclipse through the small park and came out the other side, on a street that ran along the river. Then he walked about three blocks back the way they had come, toward the bridge. There he mounted up, and rode Eclipse up the street, as if just arriving.

He rode up to the hotel porch, keeping his attention on the man seated there. He was in his thirties, still had the bearing of a soldier, even while seated.

"I'm Clint Adams," he said, reigning in Eclipse in front of the porch. "You the man I'm supposed to meet about the crown?"

"That's right, Paul Edders is my name. Why don't you dismount so we can talk on equal ground."

Clint did and stepped up onto the porch.

"Have a seat."

Clint saw that Edders still wore his arm holster, with the flap down over his gun. He could also feel the eyes of the other men on him as he sat across from Edders.

"I have to tell you, I was surprised to find out that the Gunsmith was representing a buyer for this item."

"Item?" Clint asked. "We're talking about the Russian Crown, right?"

"That's right."

"Well," Clint said, "getting a look at it was reason enough to get involved."

"Getting a look," Edders asked, "or getting your hands on it?"

"I wouldn't know what to do with it, Mr. Edders," Clint said. "That's why I'm only representing a buyer."

"Raymond Bonner, right?"

"That's the name."

"And why isn't he here himself?" Edders asked.

Clint felt Edders knew the answer to that question, but the man was testing him.

"He lives in the East, and unfortunately, his wife just died. He has to be there for the funeral."

"Of course, of course," Edders said. "First things first."

"So, where is it?" Clint asked. "Where's the crown?"

"Where's the money?"

"We haven't even agreed on a price, yet," Clint said. "My principal will want me to examine the crown first, then contact him. That's when he'll make his offer."

"Well," Edders said, spreading his hands, "obviously I'm not walking around with it."

"Then where is it?"

"In a safe place."

"When can I see it?"

"As soon as I'm convinced you're serious about buying it."

Clint reached into his pocket, took out a letter Quincy had given him.

"What's this?" Edders asked, accepting it.

"A letter of introduction from Raymond Bonner. It explains that I'm his representative."

Edders read the letter, then passed it back.

"All right, then," he said. "We'll have to meet again. I'll have the crown, you'll have some money."

"Mr. Bonner won't pay until I've seen the crown, and we discuss terms."

"I want a down payment," Edders said. "A show of good faith. Otherwise there's no deal."

"How much of a show of good faith?" Clint asked.

Edders thought for a moment . . .

***

When Clint left the porch, mounted Eclipse and rode back down the street, the other three soldiers joined Edders on the porch. Dimitri had almost followed after Clint, but he stopped to watch.

"What happened?" Bailey demanded.

"Relax," Edders said. "We're meeting again."

"When?"

"When he comes up with some money," Edders said. "Just a down payment."

"How much of a down payment?"

***

Dimitri found Clint waiting for him by the bridge.

"How much of a down payment?" the Russian asked, after Clint told him about the meeting.

"Ten thousand dollars."

"Ten thousand American dollars?" Dimitri repeated. "Where will we obtain such a sum?"

"I'm representing the United States Government," Clint pointed out. "Let's start there."

Chapter Thirty-Two

They rode back across the bridge and returned to St. Louis. Once there, they found their way to a telegraph office, and Clint sent a long message to Washington D.C. He not only asked for the ten thousand dollars to be released to him through a St. Louis bank, but also for them to contact the Count and get them more time.

"I do not think the Count will agree to give your government more time," Dimitri said, as they stepped outside.

"We'll wait to hear if we can have the money," Clint said. "But it'll take longer to contact the Count. That is, unless you can do it."

"I know his schedule," Dimitri said. "But that was when he had the crown to exhibit."

"Still," Clint said, "if you can send some telegrams and one reaches him—"

"Da," Dimitri said. "I will do it."

"Will he listen to you and give us more time?" Clint asked. "To tell you the truth, I've lost track and I'm not sure how many days we have left."

"It is only days," Dimitri said.

"Certainly not enough time to get the crown and bring it back to him," Clint said.

"I will try to convince him," Dimitri said, "but we will have to wait here for replies."

Clint pointed to a small restaurant across the street.

"We'll tell the clerk that's where we'll be," Clint said. "After you've sent your telegrams."

"Da!" Dimitri said, and went back inside.

***

They got a table across the street and sat so they could keep an eye on the telegraph office.

"You look uncomfortable," Dimitri said.

"I don't usually sit in the window," Clint said.

"I have noticed that you normally choose a dark, back table."

"Better not to make myself a target," Clint said.

"Do you think someone in St. Louis will try to kill you?" Dimitri asked.

"I never know," Clint said, "when somebody is going to recognize me, and get it into their head to try."

"We can see everything from here," Dimitri said. "Do not worry."

"Right," Clint said.

While he ordered coffee and a piece of peach pie, the Russian went for another complete steak supper.

While they were eating, the telegraph clerk came in with a message from Washington.

"What does it say?" Dimitri asked anxiously.

"We can pick up the money at the Bank of St. Louis," Clint said.

"All ten thousand dollars?" Dimitri asked.

"Yep."

"How could they do that?" the Russian asked.

"They're making it my responsibility," Clint said. "If we lose that money and don't get the crown, I'll have to pay it back."

"Would you be able to do that?"

"I hope I don't have to try," Clint said.

"Does it say anything about more time?"

"No mention," Clint said. "I guess they didn't get through to your Count. We'll just give it some more time while you finish that meal. Maybe one of your telegrams will get through to him."

"I hope they do," Dimitri said.

***

After the meal, Dimitri had a slice of apple pie, so Clint had another piece of peach with him.

"I never asked you," Clint said, "where'd you learn to speak English? You speak it very well."

"I came to your country as a young man," Dimitri said. "Went to school in Philadelphia, learned the language, and to hate your decadent ways."

"And was that when you learned to like burnt steak suppers?" Clint asked.

"Yes, it was," Dimitri said. "It was the only thing I liked about your country, except for some of the women."

"Like that one the other night?"

"She was the kind I like." Dimitri said. "She knew what she wanted and gave me what I wanted."

"Sounds like you satisfied each other," Clint said. "Maybe you'll see her again."

"I don't know anything about her, but her name," Dimitri said. "Trench, Sylvia Trench."

"From what I saw, she was a beauty," Clint said.

"She was that," Dimitri agreed, before filling his mouth with more pie.

Chapter Thirty-Three

They took their time with the pie and coffee, hoping that yet another reply would come in. They were about to leave the restaurant and go back to the telegraph office to check when the clerk came in, again.

"Here's another answer," he said, handing it to Dimitri.

"What is it?" Clint asked.

"The Count has given us one week from today," he said, laying the telegram down. "Get the crown back to him, or he will have to send a message to the Tsar."

"And then both governments will have their international incident," Clint said.

"Da!"

"We better go and pick up that money," Clint said. "I'm supposed to meet with Edders again tomorrow at noon."

"And he will have the crown with him?"

"I don't know," Clint said, "but he's agreed to show it to me."

"And you must show him the money."

"Yes."

"I do not know these American outlaws," Dimitri admitted. "Would they be satisfied with ten thousand dollars, and try to take it from you?"

"After all this?" Clint said. "I doubt it."

"Then how much will you offer them?"

"I have no idea what the thing is really worth," Clint said. "I was hoping you'd tell me that."

"I was in charge of keeping it safe," Dimitri told him. "I do not know the actual value of it in American currency."

"Then we're going to need help with that," Clint said.

"From who?"

"I have two ideas . . ." Clint said.

***

First, they went to the St. Louis Bank, where Clint identified himself and withdrew the money. He loaded it into his saddlebags and they started to leave.

"Oh, uh, Mr. Adams," the manager said.

"I don't know how far you're going with the money, sir, but would you like an escort?"

"That's all right," Clint said. "I have an escort." He indicated Dimitri, standing at the door.

"One man?"

"He's worth any three," Clint said. "Thank you."

136

He walked to Dimitri, and together they left the bank.

"Where do we go now?" the Russian asked.

"Back to the Mayflower Hotel," Clint said. "We don't want to stay on the street with this money."

"You think someone will try to take it from us?"

"It's possible."

"How would they know we have it?"

"Have you ever heard the saying 'The Walls Have Ears?'"

"No."

"There only needs to be one person in that bank who might pass along the information," Clint said. "We're better off hunkering down in our hotel until the meeting tomorrow."

"As you will," Dimitri agreed.

***

They made one more stop at the telegraph office. Not finding any more responses, they left word with the operator that they'd be at the Mayflower Hotel.

Once they got there, they decided to stay in one room together. Dimitri dragged the mattress from his bed down the hall to Clint's room.

"I do not intend to sleep on the floor," he said, "or share a bed with you."

"Good to hear."

Clint stowed his saddlebags filled with the cash beneath the bed.

"What will we do as far as eating?" Dimitri asked.

"One of us can go down to the dining room and bring the food up here," Clint said.

"While the other remains here with all that money," Dimitri said.

"Yes."

"So who stays and who goes?" Dimitri asked.

What Dimitri was asking was, which of them could be trusted with all that money.

"I'll go and get the food," Clint said.

Dimitri looked surprised.

"You would trust me here with the money?"

"Yes."

"Why?" the Russian asked.

"Because the crown means more to you than money," Clint said.

"And you?"

"Neither one of them means very much to me," Clint said. "I'm just trying to return the crown to the Count, where it belongs."

Chapter Thirty-Four

Clint went down to the dining room and ordered the steak dinners that he could take with him.

"Of course, sir," the waiter said. "Coming up."

While Clint waited by the doorway for the food, he saw a woman sitting alone across the room. She smiled and waved, and he recognized her as the woman who similarly waved at him from Dimitri's bed. He simply nodded back, but remained where he was. After a few moments, she stood and walked across the room to him.

"You're Dimitri's friend," she said.

Close up she was a tall, full-bodied, raven haired beauty with porcelain skin and blue eyes.

"That's right."

"He called you . . . Clint?"

"And you are Sylvia . . . Trench, was it?"

"That's right. Where is he?"

"He's upstairs," Clint said. "We decided to take our meal in our rooms."

"Then I suppose Dimitri has no time for me tonight?" she asked.

"I don't think so."

She smiled.

"And what about you, handsome?"

"Me? I'm waiting to eat."

"And after that?"

"Sleep."

She moved closer to him.

"I can't tempt you?" she asked.

"Any other time, maybe," Clint said. "but right now, I'm not willing to fight Dimitri for you."

"So take me to him," she said, "and we'll let him decide."

The waiter came over and handed Clint a tray of food, along with two mugs of beer, which he had to balance.

"I can at least carry those for you," Sylvia said, pointing to the beers.

"I think I'll be able to handle it, thanks," Clint said.

She smiled again.

"Then at least tell Dimitri I'm here," she said. "Maybe he'll want to come down and have a drink with me."

"Maybe he will."

She turned and went back to her table.

Clint went to the front desk.

"Do you have a guest named Sylvia Trench?" Clint asked.

"When would she have registered, sir?"

"Let's say in the past week?"

The clerk turned pages in the register and then said, "No, no one by that name."

"Thank you."

Clint carried the tray upstairs, kicked the door until Dimitri opened it.

"Ah, good," he said. "I am both hungry and thirsty." He lifted one beer mug from the tray and took a drink.

Clint walked to the table in the room and set the tray down, then pulled over the two chairs that went with it. He and Dimitri sat and started to eat.

"Burnt," Clint said, "just the way you like it."

"Excellent."

"I saw your friend downstairs."

"My friend?"

"Sylvia Trench," Clint said. "She wanted to come up."

"And you told her no, of course."

"Of course."

From his vantage point, Clint could see the saddlebags under the bed. He had to assume the money was still in them. To check it would show Dimitri he didn't trust him. And he did. Almost.

"What did she say?"

"She offered herself to me, instead," Clint said.

"And you turned her down?"

"I did," Clint said. "I told her I wouldn't fight you for her."

"You would not have to," Dimitri said. "She can be yours."

"That's all right," Clint said. "We have enough to do without getting involved with her."

"You would enjoy her," Dimitri said. "I did."

"Oh, I don't doubt that," Clint said. "I don't doubt that, at all."

***

Sylvia Trench saw her boss enter the dining room, then walk to her table and sit with her.

"Where are they?"

"Upstairs," Sylvia said. "Adams came down and brought food up for them."

"Then they have something up there worth guarding," her boss said.

"That's what I figure."

"So," the boss said, "All we have to do is go up and take it."

"Just you and me?"

At that moment, four men appeared in the doorway.

"No," the boss said, "not just us."

Chapter Thirty-Five

They were finishing their meal when Clint stopped with the fork halfway to his mouth.

"What is it?" Dimitri asked.

"Let's get behind these mattresses," Clint said.

"Why?"

"I hear the floorboards out in the hall."

"But my steak—"

"Just do it!" Clint hissed.

Dimitri picked his mattress up from the floor, and Clint pulled his off the bed. Then they palmed their guns and waited.

"I hear nothing," Dimitri whispered.

"Wait!" Clint snapped.

And then Dimitri heard the floorboards as well, just outside the door. He didn't doubt Clint's hearing any longer.

Suddenly, something impacted the door and it snapped open. Two men with guns appeared, with two more behind them. Their obvious intention was to rush into the room, spread out and start shooting. They didn't get the chance. Clint and Dimitri shot the first two, and when they fell to the floor, they shot the other two surprised men. That left two dead men in the room, and two in the hall.

And then there were excited guests in the hall, demanding to know what was going on.

"Go back to your rooms," Clint called out to them. "Everything's under control."

Slowly the people returned to the safety of their own rooms. Then the desk clerk appeared and came running down the hall.

"What happened?" he asked.

"These four men broke into my room and tried to kill us," Clint said. "We had to defend ourselves."

"Oh God," the clerk said. "I'll have to explain this to the owner, and the law."

"When the law gets here, send them up," Clint said. "And as far as anyone in the lobby is concerned, we're dead."

"What?"

"I'm guessing whoever sent those four up here is still down there," Clint said. "I want them to think they succeeded."

"I see," the clerk said, looking confused.

"Just send the law up here and we'll talk to them," Clint said.

"Yes, sir."

"And remember," Clint said. "We're dead."

As the clerk left, Clint and Dimitri dragged all four bodies into the room.

"What do we do now?" Dimitri asked.

"Let's take your mattress back to your room and put it on your bed," Clint said. "I'll bring my mattress, and the saddlebags."

"That is wise, since we can no longer lock this door."

They moved down the empty hall, not seeing anyone, and with no one seeing them. Along the way Clint was able to steal a peek into the saddlebags, where the money still sat.

Once they were in Dimitri's room, Clint started to lock the door, but the Russian said, "Wait!"

He ran back to Clint's room, returning with the remainder of their meals.

"Good thinking," Clint said, locking the door.

They sat down to finish eating, with their guns at their sides.

***

The next time Clint heard the floorboards creaking in the hall, it was followed by a knock at the door. Dimitri grabbed his gun, but Clint held a hand out to him to stay his reaction.

Clint walked to the door, carrying his gun.

"Yes?"

"Is that Mr. Adams?"

"Yes."

"Lieutenant Daly, here, St. Louis Police."

Clint opened the door a crack. The tall, fortyish man showed him his badge, and Clint opened the door the rest of the way.

"This is Lieutenant Colonel Dimitri Markovich," Clint said, "of the Russian army."

"Really," Daly said. "Now that's interesting. Can you also explain to me why there are four dead men in your room?"

"We can try," Clint said. "Have a seat. We don't have anything to offer you to drink."

"That's okay," Daly said. "Just get on with it."

***

After Clint had finished talking, and Dimitri finished eating, Daly stared at them.

"So, this Lesser Imperial Crown of Russia is worth a lot?" he asked.

"Yes," Clint said.

"And they were trying to steal it from you," Daly said, "even though you don't have it yet."

"They were after what they could get, I'm sure," Clint said. "The crown, or some money."

"And you have ten thousand dollars?"

"Da!"

Daly looked at Clint.

"Yes," he said.

"Here in this room?"

"Yes," Clint said.

"Is that wise?"

"Where else would you have me put it?" Clint asked.

"You could've left it in the bank until morning," Daly said. "Why do I think you kept the money here as bait? Did you know these four men?"

"Never saw them before in our lives," Clint said.

"Do you have any idea who might've sent them?"

"Not really," Clint said. "It could've been someone who knew we took the money from the bank, or somebody just out to make a reputation for themselves."

"By killing the Gunsmith, you mean."

"Yes."

"And your Russian friend, he would have been . . . an innocent bystander?"

"I'm afraid so."

"Well," Daly said, "I'm having the bodies removed as we speak. If you'll stop by my office in the morning and make a statement, we should be all right."

"We'll do that," Clint said.

"Good-night, then," Daly said, and left.

"So much for your local law enforcement," Dimitri said.

"He may not have heard from Washington yet," Clint said, "but he will tomorrow. Then we can move on to our meeting. For now, let's get some sleep."

"As long as no one else tries to kill us."

Chapter Thirty-Six

In the morning they rose early so Clint could send a telegram to Washington D.C. Then they went to the St. Louis Police Department building and asked for Lieutenant Daly. The policeman told them, "You can go."

"What?"

"We don't need anything from you," Daly said. "As you probably know, we heard from Washington, and you're free to go."

"What did the message from Washington say?" Clint asked.

"Something that made my superiors very unhappy," Daly said. "It said not to delay you in any way."

"I'm sorry, Lieutenant," Clint said. "It's just that we have a job to do."

"We all do," the Lieutenant said. "So you go and do yours, and I'll do mine."

"Agreed," Dimitri said.

He and Clint left, mounted their horses and once again rode for St. Charles.

***

"You've had that in here the whole time?" Bailey asked Edders.

The four ex-soldiers stared at the crown sitting on the bed in Edders' room.

"Where else would I leave it?" Edders asked. "With Quincy?"

"I wouldn't trust him," Lee said.

"Exactly."

Edders wrapped the crown in a cloth and placed it in the sack they had brought along for just that purpose.

"Are you really gonna show it to Adams?" Bailey asked.

"How else do we convince him we have it?" Edders asked. "And get the down payment?"

"And what stops him from just takin' it?" Bailey asked.

"You three will have your guns on him," Edders said.

"You know," Gillespie said, "if we killed him, we'd all be famous."

The other three looked at him.

"I don't want to be famous," Edders said. "I want to be rich."

"I gotta agree with that," Lee said. "I prefer rich to famous."

"You're an idiot," Bailey said.

"All right," Edders said, "I'll take this downstairs with me. Take up the same positions you had yesterday."

"What about dynamite?" Gillespie asked.

The other three looked at him again.

"What?" Edders asked.

"We tie a stick of dynamite to the crown," Gillespie said. "If he tries to take it from us, we blow it up."

"Blow the crown to pieces?" Edders asked.

Gillespie nodded.

"And kill the Gunsmith," he added.

"You're an idiot," Bailey said. "We're not blowin' up the crown. Not after all we've gone through for it."

"And we're not killing the Gunsmith," Edders said. "At least, not until he pays us."

"So we might kill 'im?" Gillespie asked, hopefully.

"We'll see," Edders said. "First things first. Let's make our deal for this crown. That's what we've been waiting for."

***

Clint and Dimitri retraced their steps, which left the Russian in the park across the street from the hotel, with Clint's rifle. Then Clint did what he had done the day before, so it would look as if he was just riding in. When he did, he saw Edders on the porch.

Clint dismounted, dropped Eclipse's reigns to the ground, and stepped up onto the porch. This time Edders had a pitcher of something on a table next to him, and two glasses.

"Lemonade?" he asked.

"Why not?"

Clint sat and accepted a glass. Underneath Edders' chair was a sack.

"Is that it?" he asked.

"Where's the down payment?"

"In my saddlebags."

"Get it," Edders ordered.

"Let me see the crown," Clint said.

"Only after I've seen the money."

Clint took a sip of his drink, then set the glass down, walked to Eclipse, and reached into one saddle bag. He removed one bound bundle of bills and took it onto the porch.

He handed the bills to Edders, who saw the bank binding around it.

"This is not ten thousand," he said.

"The rest is in my saddlebags," Clint promised.

"I wish I could hand you a piece of the crown, but . . ."

Edders pulled the sack from beneath his chair, opened it far enough for him to partially unfold the cloth inside.

Clint saw the gleam of gold, and the twinkle of some gems.

"Good enough?" Edders asked.

"I'm afraid not," Clint said. "I've got to see the whole crown."

"And I've got to see the whole down payment," Edders said.

"All right."

Clint got the saddlebags and brought them up onto the porch.

"Here," he said, holding them out to Edders.

The man went through the bags, counting the money, then looked at Clint.

"All there?" Clint asked.

"It's all here."

Edders reached beneath his chair, brought the bag out and set it on the table, then took the cloth covered object out. When he unwrapped it, Clint found himself looking at what he assumed was The Lesser Imperial Crown of Russia. Its gold gleamed, the jewels sparkled, and the pearls glowed.

"Good enough?" Edders asked.

"I suppose," Clint said.

Edders wrapped it and put it back in the bag, then set the bag under his chair.

"Suppose we talk price, now," he said.

Chapter Thirty-Seven

From his vantage point, Dimitri could see the other three soldiers, all of whom were spread out around the porch, but close enough to hear what was being said. He kept the rifle trained on the porch, so he could move the barrel at a moment's notice if he needed to.

He could see one of the men inching closer as if he was nervous. He decided this would be the first one he would shoot, if the shooting started.

***

Bailey, the ex-Sergeant, may have been the most experienced soldier of the four, but he was also the most impatient. Although he was able to hear the conversation on the porch very clearly, he kept moving closer and closer, almost an inch at a time. The second time Adams went to his horse for the saddlebags, he almost reacted badly, which would have blown the whole deal.

If things didn't go right, Bailey was very close to stealing the crown for himself. He knew if he had to dispose of it, he would get a lot less, but not having to split the proceeds would have made that worthwhile.

Several times he almost drew his gun, but held back.

***

"Fifty thousand?" Edders repeated. "Is that a joke?"

"No joke," Clint said. "A jumping off point."

"Well, I suggest you jump further," Edders said. "Believe me, I consider ten thousand dollars a small down payment."

"I can go as high as seventy-five thousand," Clint said.

"Go higher."

"A hundred, then," Clint said. "That's the highest I'm authorized to go."

"When would we get the money?" Edders asked.

"I just have to send a telegram, then pick the money up at the bank."

"So, a day or two?"

"If that," Clint said. "Do you think you can wait that much longer?"

Edders put his hand on the saddlebags with ten thousand dollars in them.

"I think we might be able to muddle through until then," he answered.

Chapter Thirty-Eight

Clint and Dimitri rode back to the bridge, where they dismounted, and Clint told the Russian about the meeting.

"One hundred thousand dollars?" Dimitri asked. "That is a lot, no?"

"Yes, it's a lot," Clint said.

"Would your government pay that much?"

"I don't think so," Clint said, "but how about yours?"

"My government will not pay for what is already theirs," Dimitri said.

"That's what I thought you'd say."

"We should return to the hotel and take the crown back," Dimitri suggested.

"I thought we'd make a plan—"

"There may not be time."

"I know," Clint said, "but we did take care of four would be thieves last night. It might take a while for them to come up with more men."

"I do not think that will be a problem for them," Dimitri said. "We knew the other three thieves would be watching your meeting, correct?"

"Yes."

"There were two more," Dimitri said.

"Two more thieves watching?"

"No," Dimitri said, "I believe the two men I saw were watching you and the thieves. And I believe they are Russian."

"You have some of your Russian soldiers here?" Clint asked.

"No," Dimitri said, "they are not my men."

"Then whose are they?"

"Probably a man named Ali Karim Bey," Dimitri said.

"Bey? Is that a Russian name?"

"No, it is Turkish," Dimitri said. "Bey is a thief who has long coveted the Russian crown. I believe he followed us here, intending to steal it."

"And you just decided to tell me that now?"

"To be truthful, I did not think Bey was here until last night."

"Why last night?"

"Because the four men we killed were Russian."

"And when were you going to tell me *that*?"

"I thought I would wait and see what happened with the meeting today," Dimitri admitted. "I thought perhaps we might recover the crown today."

"So do you think this Ali Karim Bey is planning on taking the crown from the thieves, or from us?"

"Well, there are four thieves and two of us," Dimitri said. "And he has already lost four men—"

"Wait a minute," Clint said, cutting Dimitri short. "Why would the four Russians last night try to steal ten thousand dollars from us if what they wanted was the crown?"

"I do not know," Dimitri admitted. "Perhaps Bey's men decided that would be easier for them. With ten thousand dollars, they would not have to return to Turkey."

"So you suspect Bey and his men will strike today and try to take a crown from Edders and his men."

"Da," Dimitri said. "And hopefully they have not already done so."

"Then we better get back there," Clint said, "and snatch the thing, ourselves."

"Da," Dimitri said. "That is a good plan."

As they mounted up Clint asked, "Are there any more secrets you might want to share with me?"

"Not a secret, exactly," Dimitri said.

"And what's that?"

"I now believe that Sylvia Trench was probably working for Ali Karim Bey when she approached me and came to my room."

"Great," Clint said, "so we have to worry about his men here, and maybe her and some more men at our hotel."

"If they attempt to steal it here and fail," Dimitri said, "they would most certainly try to take it from us."

"And how many men do you think Bey and Trench have?" Clint asked.

"That would depend on how many of your country-men they have recruited."

"I guess we should go and find out."

***

Ali Karim Bey looked out at the Missouri River as his two men approached.

"So?" he asked.

"It is there," one of them said.

"Markovich and the other?"

"Gone," the man said. "They plan to return with the money to buy the crown."

"Good," Bey said. "Then before they can purchase it, we will take it. Where are the men?"

"Waiting not far from here," the man said.

"American mercenaries?"

"Yes," the man said, "and the remainder of our men."

"Turks and Russians," the other man said. "We should have no trouble."

"Excellent," Bey said, turning to face them. "Then let's do it."

Together, they walked away from the river's edge.

Chapter Thirty-Nine

Edders and his men got back to his room with the crown, and he filled them in on what they might not have heard.

"Fifty thousand?" Bailey asked. "Is that all he offered?"

"It was all he was authorized to offer," Edders lied.

"And you agreed?" Bailey asked.

"I thought it was time to get this over with," Edders said. "So yes, I agreed."

"When do we get it?" Bailey asked.

"A day, maybe two."

"And what do we do until then?" Lee asked.

"We wait," Edders said.

As the others turned their attention away from him, he drew his gun.

***

Clint and Dimitri rode back to the St. Charles Hotel and dismounted in front of it. They ran up onto the porch and into the lobby. As they did, they heard shots, and six men turned to face them.

"Down!" Clint shouted. He grabbed Dimitri and dragged him to the floor as the men began to fire at them. The desk clerk was already on the floor.

Clint rolled one way, and Dimitri the other, both seeking cover. As they did, they drew their weapons. Clint was able to overturn a lobby divan and get behind it, while Dimitri did the same with an overstuffed armchair.

The six men also sought cover, behind the desk, around corners, behind some furniture. Clint was determined that none of those men would make it up the stairs to the next level where the guest rooms were. He could only assume they were headed for Paul Edder's room, and the crown.

As one man broke cover and headed for the stairs, Clint shouted to Dimitri, "Don't let any of them make the stairs!"

Both he and Dimitri cut the man down before he could reach the stairway.

The other five men fired at them, hot chunks of lead slamming into the divan and armchairs.

Clint and Dimitri fired back, and then Clint realized how thinly constructed the front desk was.

"Fire at the desk!" he yelled. He and Dimitri did just that, emptying their guns. As they both reloaded, the desk fell over, revealing two dead men behind it.

That left three.

The shooting stopped for a few moments as everyone examined their situation. Then one of the men said something in a language Clint didn't understand.

"Was that Russian?" he asked Dimitri.

"Turkish," Dimitri said, "They're Ali Karim Bey's men."

"That one!" Clint shouted, as another man broke for the staircase. The other two tried to lay down covering fire, so Clint left the man to Dimitri and fired at the other two. The runner made it to the stairs, but Dimitri got him before he could ascend one or two steps. The man fell back to the floor.

"One for each of us now," Clint said.

That's when they heard shots from upstairs.

"Damn it, somebody must have got up a back way," Clint said. "Can you handle these two?"

"What will you be doing?"

"I've got to get upstairs. Cover me?"

"Go!"

Clint broke from cover and ran. When he got upstairs, he realized he didn't know Paul Edders' room number, but that didn't matter. There were guests in the hall wondering what all the shooting was about.

"Get back to your rooms!" Clint yelled.

As people rushed away and slammed their doors, Clint moved along the hall, listening intently. But there was no reason for that. Eventually, there was only one open door left.

Aware there was still shooting going on downstairs, he rushed to the open door, pressed his back to the wall, listened, then stepped out into the doorway with his gun held out.

There was no need.

As he entered, he saw one man sprawled across the bed, the bedclothes soaking his blood. Beyond the bed a second man was lying on the floor, in a spreading pool of blood. He made a quick search of the room, but did not find the crown.

Suddenly, it was silent, and he heard footsteps in the hall. He turned to the door to find Dimitri bursting in, gun ready.

"Easy," Clint said. "It seems to be over. Do you know either of these men?"

Dimitri went to them, lifted their heads by their hair so he could see their faces.

"This one was the sergeant on the train," he said, pointing to the man on the bed.

"That's what I was afraid of," Clint said.

Chapter Forty

They decided not to wait around for the law.

As they left the hotel and mounted up, people were watching from the windows, so they knew the local law would get some kind of description. But they didn't have time to spend making any explanations.

Obviously the thieves had fallen out, even as Ali Karim Bey's men entered the hotel, Edders and one other had made off with the crown. Their only option now was to wait to hear from them through the dealer, Quincy.

According to Dimitri, Ali Karim Bey was not among the dead in the lobby, so he was still out there, probably with additional men. And since they didn't know where Edders and his man had gone, they might end up coming for Clint and Dimitri.

But the Mayflower Hotel was the only place Clint could think for them to go and wait, even if the place ultimately suffered the same fate as the St. Charles Hotel—with a lobby shot to pieces.

It was their only option, for the moment . . .

***

When they reached the Mayflower, they put their horses up in a livery and entered the lobby. As they headed for the stairs, the desk clerk hailed them.

"I'm sorry, Mr. Adams," he said. "Uh . . ."

"Spit it out," Clint said.

"You don't have rooms anymore."

"We did not check out," Dimitri pointed out.

"With all the damage that was done, the manager made me check you both out," the clerk said.

"Well," Clint said, "you can check us right back in."

"But the manager—"

"I'll take care of the manager," Clint said. "Just give us one room, this time. That way if there is more damage, it'll be to a single room."

That didn't seem to make the clerk feel any better, but he went ahead and gave them a key.

"If the manager gives you a hard time, send him to me," Clint said, accepting the key.

"I will, sir."

Clint and Dimitri went up to the room and found that the clerk had given them a larger room with two beds.

The first thing Clint did was look out the window.

"We're looking down at the main street," he complained, "but at least there's no access."

Dimitri came to the window.

"There could be someone with a rifle on the roof across the street," he said.

"If there is," Clint said, "we'll get him before he can get away. Let's just stay away from the window as much as possible."

There was a table and two chairs near the window, which they moved across the room so they would be able to eat there without danger of being picked off.

Clint sat down heavily on one of the beds.

"I don't usually drink whiskey," he said, "but I could use one, about now."

"Would vodka do?" Dimitri asked, taking a bottle from his saddlebag. It looked almost full.

"You've had that this whole time?" Clint asked.

"Just for emergencies," Dimitri said.

"From the look of it, you haven't run into too many of those."

"Russian vodka must be enjoyed," Dimitri said, handing Clint the bottle. He took a large swallow and then handed it back. "It is usually better ice cold," the Russian added, taking a swig himself and then corking the bottle and tucking it away. "How was it?"

"It did the trick," Clint said, feeling the vodka warm his insides. "Thank you."

"Pozhaluysta."

"You know," Clint said, "I've had a question going through my mind since last night."

"What is that?"

"How did those men know what room we were in last night?" Clint said.

"The desk clerk?"

"I asked him last night. He said no one had asked for us. So they already knew. And who knew what rooms we were in?"

Dimitri frowned.

"Sylvia Trench knew which room you were in," Clint said. "Did you tell her what room I was in?"

"I did not."

Clint thought back. He had not told any of the dealers what room he was in, except for Prescott and Quincy. Prescott so he could notify them when he had a buyer. And Quincy so he knew where to find Clint if something came up concerning the buy. Clint felt sure that Prescott was on the up-and-up. And why would Quincy tell the Russians when he was working with Edders to make the sale?

Unfortunately, that left one other person.

Chapter Forty-One

After Clint told Dimitri who he suspected and what he wanted to do, Dimitri said, "So you don't want to just wait for them to contact us, again."

"After what happened today, maybe they won't," Clint said.

"But Edders will still want to sell the crown," Dimitri said. "Especially since he has killed two of his own. That means he only has to divide the money two ways, not four."

"What if he thinks we sent the men in the lobby?" Clint asked. "I mean they were Russian and Turkish, right?"

"How would he know that?" Dimitri said. "He was upstairs killing his partners."

"Good point. Okay, then, let's split up. You wait here for contact, and I'll go and see the lady."

"You think she will confess?" Dimitri asked.

"If she's involved and wants her cut, she will," Clint said. "She'll want to make her own deal. In any case, if I can convince her not to send any more men after us, we can concentrate on Edders and his man."

"You believe she is working with Ali Karim Bey?"

"He'd need an American contact, wouldn't he?"

"Da, he would."

"So let's find out if it's her."

***

Clint left the Mayflower and took a horse drawn cab to the gallery. As he entered, Dakota Wood looked over at him and smiled, then went back to talking with her customer. Clint looked around until she was finished and the man left.

"Hello, you," she said. "What brings you here?"

"The crown," Clint said.

"Oh," she said, "so this is business?"

"It is."

She folded her arms.

"So if you have something to ask me, ask."

"Last night four men kicked in my door and tried to kill me," he said.

"That's terrible."

"I'm trying to find out how they knew what room I was in," he said.

"They asked the desk clerk?"

"He says no."

She shrugged.

"He lied?"

"I don't think so."

"Who knew what room you were in?"

"You did," Clint said. "I was dumb enough to tell you."

"Because you secretly wanted me to come there," she said. "And now you're mad that I didn't."

"That's not it," Clint said. "I'm mad because you sent four Russians to kill me."

"Why would I do that, Clint?" she asked, looking very innocent—too innocent. She was one of those women who lied with her eyes wide.

"Because you want the crown," he said. "I figured the men were breaking into my room because they realized I had picked up some money from the bank. But that wasn't it. You just wanted to get rid of us so you could make an offer on the crown. Or somehow steal it for yourself." Then he asked the question he wanted to ask, and watched her eyes get wider. "Do you know a man named Ali Karim Bey?"

When she lied and said, "No," he thought her eyes would pop out.

"You're a terrible liar, Dakota," Clint said. "Give Bey a message. Tell him if he crosses my path again, I'll kill him."

"Clint—"

"Don't," he said, cutting her off. "That big, wide-eyed look isn't going to work. This is the only way it figures."

Clint turned and walked out.

***

Outside the gallery, he decided to wait a while and see who came out after him, so he crossed the street and found a cozy doorway to watch from.

***

After Clint left, another person came out of the back room.

"You heard?"

"Everything," Sylvia Trench said. "You know, he's right. You are a terrible liar."

"Never mind that!" Dakota snapped. "You've got to get to Bey."

"I will," Sylvia said, coming around the counter, "but I have something else to do first."

"What's that?"

As she reached Dakota, she took a knife from her belt and slid it neatly between the gallery owner's ribs. Her eyes fluttered and she fell into Sylvia's arms.

"This," Sylvia Trench said, and lowered Dakota's lifeless body to the floor.

Chapter Forty-Two

When no one came out after fifteen minutes, Clint became impatient. He crossed back over to the gallery and tried the front door, found it locked. He didn't like that. He peered in through the window, saw nobody. He wondered if Dakota had gone out the back door.

He made his way around the building, found that it did, indeed, have a back door. There was no window, so he simply put his shoulder to the door and shoved. It was amazing how many businesses had solid front doors, and flimsy back ones. The door popped open.

He worked his way through the back room to the curtained doorway, and into the gallery. There he smelled the blood right away, found Dakota on the floor behind the counter. Apparently, she had gotten herself mixed up in something she couldn't handle.

But now he was worried about Dimitri, back at the Mayflower alone. He left by the back door and headed for the hotel.

***

When the knock came at the door, Dimitri thought Clint might have forgotten his key. But he went to the door with his gun, anyway. When he opened it, he was surprised to see Sylvia Trench standing there. The dark-haired beauty smiled at him.

"Did you think you could get away from me by switching rooms?" she asked.

"What makes you believe I wanted to get away from you?" he said. "Come in."

She entered the room, the aroma of her perfume engulfing him. She walked to the center of the room and turned.

"This is much better," she said. "There is more room for us to . . . play in."

She was wearing a blue dress with a short jacket over it. The dress was belted at the waist.

"Do you think you're going to need that gun?"

"Oh yes," he said, "I am definitely going to need this gun."

She pouted and said, "Dimitri—"

"Did Ali Karim Bey think I would succumb to your feminine wiles twice?" he asked.

She grinned.

"What man wouldn't?" she asked.

"I did once," he told her. "I will not again."

"Why not?" she asked, starting to move closer.

He pointed his gun at her.

"I do not think I would survive it," he said. "What do you have in your belt?"

She stared at him, taking a step back.

"Remove it and drop it to the floor," he said.

She took a knife from her belt and dropped it.

"Ah, a silent killer," he said. "Please raise your hands."

As she did, the door opened, and Clint came rushing in. He stopped when he saw them, and then his eyes went to the knife on the floor.

"She just killed Dakota Wood," he told Dimitri. "I think she was getting rid of the competition."

"Or a partner who was no longer useful," she said.

"And what about your other partner?" Clint asked. "Ali Karim Bey? Or is he your employer?"

"What's the difference?" she asked. "May I lower my hands? I have no other weapons."

"Wait." Clint stepped forward and searched her.

"You should have taken me up on my offer," she said to him. "We would have at least had fun. Ask Dimitri."

Clint stepped back and stood next to the Russian.

"How many men does Bey have left?" Dimitri asked.

"I suppose that depends on how many you've killed," Sylvia said.

"I count ten," Clint said.

Her eyebrows went up.

"That many? He doesn't have a lot left, then."

"And where are Edders and the crown?" Clint asked.

"I don't know," she said. "Wasn't he in St. Charles this morning?"

"He was until the shooting started," Clint said. "Then he killed two of his partners and ran."

"Ah, the thieves fell out, huh?"

"You should know all about that," Clint said, "considering what you did to Dakota Wood."

"The problem with her was that she wasn't a thief," Sylvia said. "She was going against type and doing it badly. You, yourself, said she was a terrible liar."

"So you killed her for that?"

"Mr. Bey doesn't want to leave behind too many loose ends," she said.

"Wouldn't that include you?" Clint asked.

"Not likely," she said, with a smile. "So what would you boys like to do now?"

Dimitri and Clint looked at each other.

"I can't just sit and wait," the Russian said.

"Then we might as well go and see Quincy," Clint said. "He must know a way to get in contact with Edders."

Chapter Forty-Three

They didn't know what to do with Sylvia Trench, so they took her with them.

"We're walking out of here," he told her, as they went down to the lobby. "If you try to get away, I'll shoot you down."

"Believe me," Sylvia said, "I've got no place to go."

They walked her across the lobby and out the front door.

"Stay here with her," Clint said to Dimitri. "I'll get us a cab."

"All right," Dimitri said.

"If she tries to get away, shoot her."

"I will."

As Clint walked away, Sylvia looked at Dimitri and asked, "You will?"

"Yes."

She fell silent.

***

It was the first time Clint had been to the Quincy Gallery, since originally meeting the man in a restaurant. It was in the Clayton area, just a few blocks away from the

Prescott place. As impressive as Calvin Prescott's gallery was. This one was slightly larger.

There were several people there, one at the counter talking with Quincy, and the others browsing.

Quincy looked over at them, and Clint thought he saw something in the man's face, maybe because Sylvia Trench was with them.

Clint decided not to wait until the other customers left the gallery. Maybe their presence would make Quincy more cooperative.

He approached the desk with Sylvia behind him and Dimitri bringing up the rear.

"All right, Mr. Appleton," Quincy was saying, "I'll see what I can find."

The tall, scholarly looking man turned, seemed surprised to see the three of them standing there, then said, "'scuse me," and went around them to the door.

"Mr. Adams," Quincy said, "can you wait until I take care of these other customers?"

"I don't think so, Mr. Quincy," Clint said. "I think we need to talk now."

The man stroked his long, angular jaw, then said, "All right. What is it?"

"You heard what happened in St. Charles?" Clint asked.

Quincy stared at him, then asked, "Did it go wrong?"

"Edders is on the run with the crown," Clint said. "There are Russians and Turks after him."

"Turks?"

"A man named Ali Karim Bey. Do you know him?"

"What? Ali Ka—what?"

"Edders also killed two of his own men," Clint said. "I assume he wanted to cut down on the split."

"Look," Quincy said, "I don't know what's going on—"

"You have to know, Quincy," Clint said. "You're Edders' contact."

"Look, I don't know what this is all about," Quincy said. "I'm just a middleman."

The browsers looked over, saw Dimitri, sensed something was going on, and hurriedly left.

"Turn that open sign to closed, Dimitri," Clint told him.

"It's almost closing time, anyway," Quincy said. "Do you want me to come someplace with you?"

"No," Clint said.

"I will look in the back," Dimitri said.

"Be careful," Clint said.

Dimitri bumped into a vase on a stand, knocked it over. It smashed into a million pieces when it hit the floor.

"Oops," he said, and went to the back room.

"Oh, God," Quincy bawled, "that was priceless."

Dimitri stopped in front of the doorway, peered in before stepping through. He came back in moments.

"Someone was back there," he said.

"When we came in?" Clint asked.

"There is a chair that is still warm."

Clint looked at Quincy.

"If you lie to me," he said, "this Russian is going to be like a bull in a china shop."

"Oh no . . ."

"Start with that piece of crystal," Sylvia said, pointing. "It's very valuable."

Dimitri walked over to the sculpture she was talking about. He couldn't tell what it was, but it glinted in what was left of the light coming through the front window.

He put his hand on it.

"No, no, please," Quincy shouted. "Wait. What do you want to know?"

"Where are Edders and the crown," Clint said. "How much have you told Ali Karim Bey?"

"I don't know where Edders and the crown are, now," Quincy said.

"But they were in your back room when we walked in," Clint said.

"Yes."

"And Bey?"

179

"I don't know Ali Karim—wait!"

Dimitri knocked the crystal statue off the stand, but caught it before it hit the ground.

"I'll ask you again," Clint said.

"Okay," Quincy said, "I know the name Bey, but I haven't spoken with him."

"He would need to have a contact here in St. Louis," Clint said. "If not you, then who?"

Quincy stared at him for a few moments, then said, "Why don't you ask her?"

Chapter Forty-Four

Clint looked at Sylvia, who just shrugged, then he looked back at Quincy.

"You tell Edders I'll be here tonight at ten o'clock," Clint said. "I'll have the money, he better have the crown."

"Ten," Quincy repeated, still watching Dimitri with the crystal in his hand. "I'll tell him."

Clint looked at Dimitri and nodded. The Russian put the crystal carefully back on its stand, then followed Clint and Sylvia out the front door.

"Why ten o'clock?" Dimitri asked. "What do we do in the meantime?"

"That's up to Sylvia," Clint said.

"Why me?" she asked.

"Because you're going to take us to Ali Karim Bey," Clint said.

"Because of what he said?" she asked.

"No," Clint said, "because I believe you're Bey's contact. In fact, I think you work for him."

"What makes you think that?"

"You've been letting us lead you around for the past hour," Clint said. "You're trying to figure out what to do, and that's because you're not in charge."

"You think I need a man to direct me?" she asked.

"That's exactly what I think," Clint said. "How do you contact Bey?"

"Adams—"

Dimitri reached out and grabbed ahold of one of Sylvia's arms.

"I must retrieve the crown," he said to her. "If you are not helping me, you are blocking me. I will not stand for that." He squeezed, with his massive hand, and she flinched. "You have only felt my strength during passion. Do you want to feel it when I am angry?"

She looked at Clint.

"He's breaking my arm!" she hissed.

"And I'll break the other one," Clint said.

"What do you want?" she asked.

"I want you to contact Bey."

"All right, all right!" she snapped, trying to pull away from Dimitri's hold. When he opened his hand she almost fell.

"I want you to send Bey a message. Tell him to be here tonight at nine thirty."

"Nine-thirty?" she repeated, rubbing her arm. "But you told Quincy ten."

"I want to finish with Bey before Edders gets here," Clint said.

"Are you going to kill him?" she asked.

"If he does not," Dimitri said, "I will!"

***

They found the nearest telegraph office and Clint went in with Sylvia and watched her write out the message he dictated. He didn't want her doing it in her own words, in case there was a signal.

When he had it the way he wanted, he said to her, "Send it."

They took it to the clerk, who tapped it out quickly.

"You gonna wait for a reply?" he asked. "I mean, it's local, and all."

There was a small saloon next door so Clint told the clerk they would be in there.

When they got outside Sylvia asked, "What if he doesn't respond? Or doesn't get it tonight?"

"You'll be in a lot of trouble," Clint said, "with us, and probably with him, because by tonight we will have recovered the crown."

"Maybe," she said, "when you do recover the crown we can talk about a split?"

"The crown will go back to Russia!" Dimitri snapped. "There will be no . . . split!"

"But I *will* buy you a drink," Clint said. "Let's go next door."

***

They were still working on their first drink each when the telegraph clerk entered. It had taken less than an hour for a reply.

"You got your answer, Miss," the clerk said, handing it to Sylvia. "I figured you would, what with it bein' local and all." He stared at her with unabashed admiration and lust. Clint assumed she was used to that.

"Thank you," Sylvia said.

Clint gave the man a coin, which made the clerk happy.

"Here," she said, handing the telegram to Clint when the clerk was gone, "this concerns you more than it does me."

Clint accepted it and read it.

"He says he'll meet you," Clint told her.

"He will bring men," Dimitri predicted.

"I'm sure he will," Clint said. "That's why we're going to be there early." He looked at Sylvia. "Finish your drink."

Chapter Forty-Five

Quincy was nervous.

Clint could see the strain on his face, and the sheen of perspiration on his forehead.

"He's going to give us away," Clint told Dimitri.

"Yes," the Russian agreed. "They will only have to look at him."

"I'll help," Sylvia said.

Both men looked over at her. She was sitting in a corner, being quiet, as she was told—up to that point—while Clint and Dimitri watched Quincy from the back room.

"How?" Clint asked.

"Bey is going to know something's wrong as soon as he sees Quincy," she said. "When that happens, I'll step out and he'll think it was because I was hiding back here."

"And then what?" Dimitri asked. "You will give us away?"

"I won't do that."

"Why not?" the Russian asked.

"Would you believe me if I said it was because of what we mean to each other?"

"No!" Dimitri said.

"Well then, maybe it's because you've got me." She shrugged. "I don't want to die."

She got up and walked to the doorway so she could look into the gallery.

"What do you think?" Clint asked Dimitri.

Before the Russian could answer Sylvia said, "You better decide quick. Ali Karim Bey just walked in."

They all looked. Clint saw a tree trunk of a man, wide and rather short, with a heavy black beard.

"He's alone," Clint said. "Why would he come alone?"

"Maybe because he trusts me?" Sylvia asked.

"If you try anything—" Clint started.

"I know," she said. "You'll kill me."

"Find out how many men he's got waiting outside," Clint said.

She started to go through the door, but Dimitri put his hand on her arm.

"Wait," he said.

Bey looked around the shop, then walked to the counter where Quincy was standing.

"Where is she?" he asked. Just in those three words Clint heard an accent he had never heard before.

"She-she'll be here," Quincy said.

"She said nine-thirty."

"Yes," Bey said, "she did."

He stared at Quincy and Clint thought the man was ready to run.

"What's wrong, Mr. Quincy?" Bey asked. "Why are you afraid?"

"Go!" Clint hissed, and Sylvia stepped through the door.

Bey heard her enter and turned.

"Ah," he said, "you are here."

"Yes, I am," Sylvia said. "Where are the rest of your men?"

"They are . . . near," Bey said.

"Really? I heard you lost a lot of them over the past two days."

"There are always more," Bey said. "What was so urgent I had to come here tonight, Miss Trench? Do you have the crown?"

"No," she said, "but it'll be here by ten."

Bey looked at Quincy.

"Is that true?"

"Edders is supposed to be here at ten," the dealer confirmed. "Whether or not he will have the crown . . ." Quincy spread his hands.

"If he doesn't have the crown, why would he come?" Bey asked.

"To discuss price with the buyer," Sylvia said.

"And who is the buyer?" Ali Karim Bey asked.

Sylvia pointed and said, "They are."

Clint and Dimitri stepped out of the back room. Clint figured even if—as he said—Bey's men were near, they were outside.

"Markovich!" Bey said, stepping back and reaching for his belt.

"Don't do that!" Clint said. "You'll force me to kill you."

Bey moved his hand away from his belt, which was straining against his portliness.

"What is this?" he demanded, not looking at anyone in particular.

"The crown will be here," Dimitri said, "but you are not getting it, Ali Karim Bey."

"I have come a long way, Markovich," Bey said. "I do not intend to leave empty-handed."

"That's too bad," Clint said, "because that's what's going to happen."

Now Bey looked at Sylvia.

"This is the man you told me about, this Western legend?" he asked.

"This is him," she said. "The Gunsmith."

"Markovich, what are you doing with this . . . this . . . American?" Bey demanded.

"Recovering the crown for Mother Russia, Ali Karim Bey," Markovich said.

Bey looked at both Quincy and Sylvia.

"So there is no buyer," he said.

"No," Quincy said.

"But the thieves, they believe there is?"

"Yes."

Bey looked at the clock on the wall.

"And they will be here in fifteen minutes?"

"Give or take a minute," Quincy said.

"Then I suppose this will all come to an end shortly," Bey said.

"For you," Dimitri said, "it is already ended."

Dimitri drew his gun and put a bullet in Ali Karim Bey's portly belly.

Chapter Forty-Six

"That shot will bring his men!" Clint complained, as Bey fell.

"Good," Dimitri said, "then we will end this once and for all."

"And it may also scare away the thieves."

"If they are early," Dimitri said, holstering his gun. "When have you known criminals and thieves to be on time?"

Clint moved to the front of the store and looked out. The street appeared empty. He turned and looked down at the dead Turk.

"He must have been lying," he said. "He has no men left."

"That's entirely possible," Sylvia Trench said. "When he first contacted me, he said he'd be bringing some men, but he wanted me to hire more."

"And you did," Clint said.

She nodded.

"So he had a collection of Russians, Turks and Americans, but at my count, it would seem you've handled them all," Sylvia said.

Clint returned to the front counter.

"We better move this body," Clint said. "Quincy, help me."

"Why not the Russian?" Quincy complained.

"Because he's going to keep an eye on Miss Trench," Clint replied. "Come on!"

Between him and the dealer, they dragged the heavy body into the back room. There was blood on the floor, so Dimitri grabbed a rug that was hanging on the wall.

"No, not that!" Quincy shouted, but it was too late. The Russian dropped it onto the puddle of blood.

"All right," Clint said, "we'll be in the back room. When Edders gets here make him show you the crown."

"Then what?" Quincy asked.

"Then the rest will be up to us."

Clint and Dimitri went into the back room with the dead body, taking Sylvia with them.

"Why did you have to do that?" Clint asked Dimitri, pointing at the body.

"He is an enemy of the Russian people," Dimitri said.

"You could've killed him later."

"Da, I could have," Dimitri said. "I did not."

"Russians are impulsive," Sylvia said. "Didn't you know that?"

"I'm finding out."

They heard the front door open and close.

"Who's that?" Clint whispered.

"That's the young one," Sylvia said. "His name is Lee."

"He does not have the crown," Dimitri said, observing the young man's empty hands.

"He's checking to see if the coast is clear," Clint said. "This is going to be up to Quincy."

"You can't leave it up to him," Sylvia said. "He's too nervous. Let me go in."

Clint and Dimitri exchanged a look, and then Clint said, "Go ahead."

She stepped through the doorway as Lee reached the front counter.

"Quincy—" Lee said, but then saw Sylvia. "Miss Trench."

"You're Lee, right?" she asked.

"Chris Lee, that's right," he said. He looked around. "Where's the buyer? The Gunsmith?"

"He'll be here," she said. "Where are Edders and the crown?"

Lee hesitated, then said, "He'll be here. I have to signal him."

"Then do it," she said.

"Edders said not until the Gunsmith gets here," Lee told her.

"There's going to be no money if the crown's not here," Sylvia said. "Signal him, or it's all off."

"She's good," Clint whispered to Dimitri.

"We will see," the Russian said.

Lee nodded, went to the front door and waved his arms. Minutes later the door opened, and Paul Edders entered, carrying the sack Clint had seen before.

He stopped just inside the door.

"Where's the buyer?" he demanded. "Where's Adams?"

"Stay here, Dimitri," Clint said.

"I will be ready," Dimitri said, taking out his gun.

Clint stepped from the back room.

"There you are," Edders said, spotting him.

Sylvia turned to look at Clint.

"Is that the crown?" Clint asked.

"It is."

"Let's see it." Clint approached the counter. Quincy shrank back, but Sylvia leaned forward as Edders put the sack on the counter.

Edders peeled down the edges of the sack, revealing the crown inside. When it came into view, they all caught their breath and stared at it.

That was when Dimitri came from the back room, waving his gun.

"Everyone must stand still!" he barked.

They all turned and looked at him.

"What're you doing?" Clint demanded.

"Just stand still!" Dimitri snapped.

They all froze, except for Sylvia, who slowly walked over and stood in front of the crown. Then, slowly, she closed the bag and lifted it from the counter.

"Not yet!" Dimitri said. "Get their guns."

Too late, Sylvia realized her mistake. She set the bag down and turned to take Clint's gun, but before she could he drew and fired. The bullet struck Dimitri dead center and his gun dropped from his hand.

At the same time Edders drew and fired, his bullet striking Sylvia. Quincy stepped back and lifted his hands, as if to ward off any bullets coming his way.

Chris Lee wasn't sure what to do, so he simply froze.

Clint and Edders turned to face each other, guns in their hands.

"Don't make a bad mistake, Edders," Clint said.

"Paul?" Chris Lee said.

"Tell the young man not to touch his gun, Edders," Clint said. "This can only end one way unless you both drop your weapons."

"And then do what?" Edders asked.

"Walk out the door, both of you," Clint said. "I'm sure you've got that ten thousand stashed somewhere. Be satisfied with that."

"You're going to let us keep that money?" Edders said, in disbelief.

"Hey, it's not my money," Clint said. "Take it and go."

Edders considered Clint's proposal, then dropped his gun and said, "Lee, do as he says."

The younger man plucked his gun from his holster and dropped it.

"Now get out," Clint said. "Have a nice life."

As nice as two deserters on the run could have, he thought, as they went out the door.

Clint looked at Quincy, who was still standing stock still, his eyes wide.

"Do you have a weapon back there?" Clint asked.

"N-no."

"Good. Just stand still."

"Yessir."

Clint went to Sylvia, saw that she was dead, then went to Dimitri, whose eyes fluttered.

"Damn you, you big stupid Russian. How long have you been planning this?"

"W-when she came to my room, we talked," Dimitri said. "She and your decadent lifestyle convinced me. I—I just watched for my chance."

"And this was it."

Dimitri laughed, and blood dripped from the corner of his mouth.

"So I thought," he said, and died.

Clint holstered his gun without replacing the one spent shell. He walked to the counter.

"Now what?" Quincy asked.

"I take this crown back to where it belongs," Clint said.

"But . . . it's worth a fortune," the dealer said.

"It's worth even more to the Tsar of Russia," Clint told him.

"B-but, what do I do with these bodies?"

"That's up to you," Clint said.

Coming June 27, 2020

THE GUNSMITH
460
The Traveling Undertaker

**For more information
visit:** www.SpeakingVolumes.us

On Sale Now!

THE GUNSMITH
458
The Gunsmith Saloon

**For more information
visit:**

On Sale Now!

THE GUNSMITH *series*
Books 430 - 457

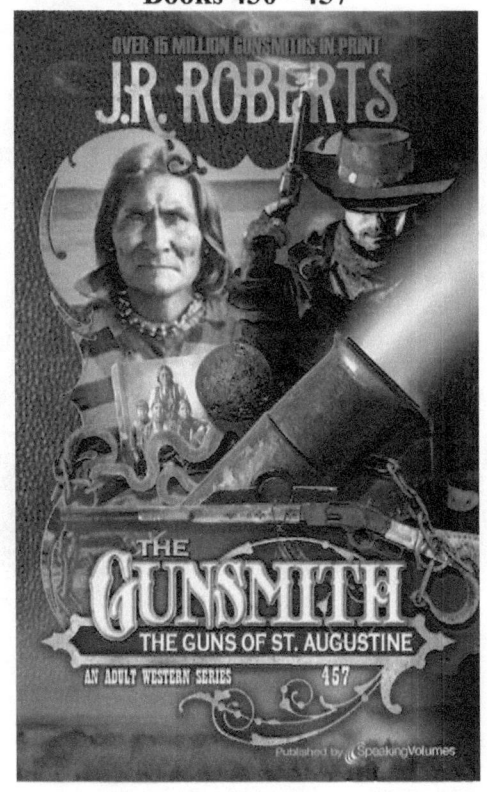

For more information
visit: www.SpeakingVolumes.us

On Sale Now!

Lady Gunsmith
Books 1 - 8
Roxy Doyle and the Silver Queen

For more information
visit: www.SpeakingVolumes.us

On Sale Now!

**Award-Winning Author
Robert J. Randisi (J.R. Roberts)**

**For more information
visit:**